Martin

DEAD MAN'S
BAY

arrow books

Published by Arrow Books in 2005

1 3 5 7 9 10 8 6 4 2

Copyright © David Ralph Martin 2004

David Ralph Martin has asserted his right under the Copyright, Designs
and Patents Act, 1988 to be identified as the author of this work

First published in the United Kingdom in 2004 by William Heinemann

Arrow Books
The Random House Group Limited
20 Vauxhall Bridge Road, London SW1V 2SA

Random House Australia (Pty) Limited
20 Alfred Street, Milsons Point, Sydney,
New South Wales 2061, Australia

Random House New Zealand Limited
18 Poland Road, Glenfield
Auckland 10, New Zealand

Random House (Pty) Limited
Endulini, 5A Jubilee Road, Parktown 2193, South Africa

Random House Group Limited Reg. No. 954009
www.randomhouse.co.uk

A CIP catalogue record for this book is available from the British Library

Papers used by Random House are natural, recyclable products made from
wood grown in sustainable forests. The manufacturing processes conform to
the environmental regulations of the country of origin

ISBN 0099278642

Typeset by SX Composing DTP, Rayleigh, Essex
Printed and bound in Great Britain by
Bookmarque Ltd, Croydon, Surrey

The March voyage was rough and the stupid bitch was dead. They slid her body over the side into the Channel twenty miles south-west of Portland and told her companions, nine of them, all young women from the Ukraine or Moldova, that she was ill and being looked after in sickbay until they reached Southampton.

In fact Irina, a fair-haired pleasant-looking Moldovan girl of nineteen, had died because five of the heroin-packed condoms in her stomach had burst when she had been thrown out of her bunk on to the steel floor during a Force 9 gale. The other forty-two condoms were still intact, so they didn't dump her until all had been recovered.

Three days later the Old Harry, a Weymouth boat longlining for bass in the race off Portland, pulled up what was left of her.

I

'Come!'

A buzzer sounded, then a click. Vic pushed the door open. Detective Chief Superintendent Sam Richardson, bull-necked, pepper-and-salt hair, face the colour of fresh veal, sat behind his desk. There was a buff file on it, closed. On the cover:

0483 V. HALLAM DET. SGT BRISTOL 'A' DIVISION

'Morning, Vic.'

'Morning, Sam.'

Sam picked up the file, turned it round and chucked it across the desk towards Vic. 'Your glorious career.' The lipless don't-think-I-mean-it smile. 'Sit yourself down, Vic.'

'Thanks.' Vic pulled up a five-wheeled typing chair. The grey cloth seat sank a couple of inches underneath him. They looked at each other: Sam, fifty, beginning to bulk out under his maroon-stripe stockbroker's shirt, and Vic, thirty-nine, well-built with a hard, pale face, grey eyes and dark straight hair. He was wearing his usual M&S charcoal suit, baggy and shiny under the thighs from years of sitting in unmarked cars.

'Thought about it, have you?'

'This sleeper business?'

'Yes.'

'Yeah.' Vic pulled out a pack of Marlboro. 'I've thought about it.'

'Well?'

'It all depends –'

'Always fucking does with you, doesn't it?'

'What I mean is, *I* know what a sleeper is, and *you* know what a sleeper is. Trouble is, are they the same thing?'

'Stroll on, Vic – I think I'm doing you a favour and you think I'm trying to con you –'

Wouldn't be the first time.

'Way I see it, Sam, a sleeper is some old bugger you send to a strange town to blend into the wallpaper. He has nothing to do with the town plod, makes out he's a bit of a chancer and hangs out with the local villains. If he hears anything, he reports back to HQ and that's it. He never breaks cover – ever.'

Sam's lipless grin. 'So?'

'I can't see you not pulling my strings.'

'Why should I do that?'

'Because you're a string-puller.'

'Fair enough.' Sam opened Vic's file and took out his Cross ballpoint. 'I'll say you're turning it down in order to take early retirement.' He clicked the end of the ballpoint, then looked up. 'It's a big job, Vic. I'm going to need all the help I can get and you're a fucking A1 thieftaker.'

Typical Sam. Blackmail first, bullshit second. Or does he know about Ellie – know you can't afford early retirement?

'Mind if I smoke?'

Sam shoved a black glass ashtray across the desk. 'Burst into flame all I care.'

'Thanks.' Vic lit up. 'Who's running the show?'

'SO22.'

'The Met?'

'Drugs boys, Customs, MI5, MI6, NCIS, half bloody Interpol – you name it, they're in it. And when push comes to shove they'll all have their snouts in the trough, all after the bloody gravy while we've done all the fucking work. They won't tell us fuck-all till they have to – meanwhile security's got more holes than granny's drawers. In other words the same old same old –'

'Yeah. What's our patch?'

'Bristol Channel, round the corner, up the South Coast as far as Poole. Then it's the Met and the rest up to the Thames.'

'Big.'

'You're not the only one, Vic.' Sam reached into his desk drawer and pulled out two yellow sheets of stapled A4. 'This is the basic bumf.' The first page was headed 'PRESS' and was dated for release in ten days' time. The second page had three neatly typed paragraphs titled 'OPERATION KINGFISHER'. The first paragraph outlined an *important new government initiative for a coordinated crackdown on crime*'; the second was about the change in drugs policy and supplying addicts direct, and the third paragraph concerned the links between illegal immigration and the supply of Class A narcotics and concluded, *'Far tougher penalties can be expected for all these forms of trafficking.'*

Vic said, 'Why tell everybody?'

'Once they open these free shooting galleries for the fucking addicts they think the dealers'll panic, flood the market. We're in deep, we catch 'em crawling out the woodwork and jump all over the fucking immigrants. Simple. Simple my arse –'

'Where do I come in?'

'You going to do it?'

'I'm still thinking about it.'

Sam said, 'You know what Thought did, don't you?'

'What?'

'Shat himself.' The lipless grin. 'While he was thinking about it.' Sam turned to pull an *AA Motorists' Atlas of Great Britain* off the shelf behind him, opened it and swivelled it round for Vic to see. Sam's thick red finger traced out a long arc of the South Coast. 'You'll be on this stretch here – Brixham to Portland, and on again to Poole.'

'It's still too big, Sam. I'd spend all day in the car.'

Sam leaned back and clasped his hands behind his neck. 'You always were an awkward fucker, Hallam.'

'Not going to pick up anything stuck in a car, am I?'

'Christ, Vic, I already told you – you won't be the only pebble on the fucking beach.'

'Meaning what?'

'Sometimes you'll work in pairs, threes if you're on all-night obbo, more if it's a bust. Happy now?'

'I still need to know where I'm based, what my home patch is.'

'*Fucking Christ, Hallam!*'

Sam stood up, walked around behind Vic and over to the corner window. Vic knew he was looking at his maroon Saab in its designated parking space with its RESERVED DET. CH. SUP. ONLY nameboard: it was what Sam did to calm down.

The back of his neck and the side of his face had gone beef-red. Hating himself, Vic said, 'Sorry, Sam.'

Sam turned round and forced a smile. 'That's all right, son.' Then, taking his seat again: 'Fuck me, I never thought I'd see the day.'

'What?'

'Vic fucking Hallam fucking apologising.' Sam shoved the atlas towards Vic. 'Which bit d'you know best?'

'Here – Lyme Bay to Portland. I've sailed it, fished it, walked the coast path one end to the other – been on holidays there since I was a kid –' Vic stopped, realising he was sounding too eager, giving Sam an arm to twist.

Sam's glance, quick as a bird. 'You must like it then?'

'It's not bad.'

A long pause, then the grin: 'So that's settled, is it? If I say that's your patch, you'll take on this assignment as sleeper for the duration of Operation Kingfisher?'

'How long's the duration?'

'As long as it takes to get results. Real results. Home Office big nobs have come up with this brilliant idea that drugs, gun crime and illegal immigration are all "interrelated". What they mean is they think there's fucking votes in it. So what we have to do is knock 'em all on the head and get rid of the black and white toerags running the fucking rackets. Could take months, could take years. Unless somebody gets fed up with it or there's another fucking election.' Sam leaned forward. 'Come on Vic, yes or no. Crunch time. Either piss or get off the pot.'

'What about money?'

'Same as it is now, you'll get the same money you do now, plus living expenses, accommodation allowance, car exes, plus an extra whack on your pension. I was you, I'd jump at it.'

'Would you?'

'What? Good as retirement on full pay, nothing to do all day but sit on your arse watching the fucking tide going in and out? Piece a piss, man. Come on, Vic –'

'There is one thing –'

'Always fucking is with you –'

'Ellie's pregnant.'

Sam, who had no children of his own and worked late to avoid going home to his Liberal councillor wife, sat back and looked at Vic. 'That the nurse you been knocking off?'

'Ellie is a nurse, yes.'

8

'What you going to do about it?'

Vic shrugged. 'Get married.'

Sam looked at Vic as if he were witnessing a fatal traffic accident. 'You poor cunt.'

2

By half past four, walking home after transferring his workload, clearing his desk and handing his clapped-out red Ford Escort back to Traffic, Vic wasn't sure whether he was walking on air or had just stepped off the cliff.

Point One was he'd taken the sleeper job, shaken Sam's sandpaper-rough hand on it: there was no going back.

Point Two was he hadn't told Ellie – apart from saying he was thinking about it. Going home now and presenting it as one of those spur-of-the-moment things wasn't going to cut much ice with Ellie. He could feel her hot blue eyes lasering through him even as he walked. He knew he needed to stop off for a large spine-stiffening vodka, but the nearest all-day boozers were miles away.

They always were when you wanted them.

He knew what she'd say. She'd say they hadn't talked it over, hadn't discussed the finances, hadn't thought about what she was going to do about her job, what they were going to do about getting married, and where, if anywhere, they were going to live.

Oh shit.

Which brought him to Point Three – he'd just rung his old mate, Joe Moore. Vic and Joe had grown up together, joined the Force together; but then Joe, who was six foot two and fifteen stone, had got stuck in uniform as a beat PC for fifteen years, so five years ago he'd quit. Now he was a fisherman, married, two kids, living in St Bride's Harbour, Dorset, halfway between Weymouth and Lyme Regis. Joe had told him there was a coastguard cottage going for long-let on the beach, fully renovated, two bed, all mod cons. And Vic phoned and faxed the agents, looked at the pictures and particulars and, in the all-powerful euphoria of the moment – one of those moments when you think God is giving you one of His rare smiles: 'Go on, My son, don't miss out on this one, I am with you, be My guest and cover yourself in glory –'

Vic had taken a year's lease on the place. Still without telling Ellie.

Shit and double shit.

Then Joe had told him he was in deep shit with the bank over falling down on repayments on the second mortgage he'd taken out to buy *Rob Roy*, a dark-blue Lochin 33 charter fishing vessel with a 250hp Volvo Penta, seventeen knots on the plane and the sweetest lines Vic had ever seen. Now the bank was threatening repossession on the boat *and* the house. So there and then, on the phone, Vic had offered Joe fifteen grand for a half share.

With Joe being an ex-copper, it was, he told himself at the time, the perfect cover.

Now he was on the way home to face Ellie and tell her he'd just spent a quarter of their joint assets on a wet dream –

And that was Point Four: the killer. Because, as you well know, Hallam, Women and Boats do not mix – they never have and never will. That's why they're both called She. And you, Hallam, are going to end up divorced before you're even fucking married.

Ellie was in the kitchen of the flat Vic had just sold because his ex-wife Trish was insisting on her sixty thousand pounds' worth of flesh. Now all their clothes and most of their joint possessions were in cardboard boxes ready to move. Ellie was still wearing her thin pale blue staff nurse's uniform. She was twenty-eight, born and trained in Birmingham, and had been a senior staff nurse at Bristol Royal Infirmary for three and a half years. When Vic came in, Ellie was at the sink washing up the breakfast things so they could use them for supper. Around her uniform she wore a broad black elasticated belt with a Victorian silver buckle in the shape of a butterfly. The belt showed off her high sturdy bust and magnificent backside. Vic stood admiring it shake from side to side as she energetically scrubbed the morning porridge off their one and only saucepan.

Watching her, Vic recalled what Harry Hill, an ex-Artillery pensioner who worked in 'A' division stores, had to say about women: 'If God made anything better, my son, you can bet He kep' it for Hisself.'

Clothed, Ellie looked pleasantly attractive: blue eyes with dark lashes, fresh complexion, nice mouth, but in her black hospital flatties maybe a little on the heavy side. Naked and straight out of the bath, as Vic never tired of seeing her, the generous solidity of her breasts and her warm pink belly and loins made Vic think first of Renoir and then, at the speed of light, of mad last-gasp fucking. They had been living together just over six months and even when they were both knackered and sleeping in a damp, sagging double bed in Bishopston while the flat was being sold, they couldn't keep their hands off each other. Ellie, now two months pregnant, knew it was a fever and would pass, but Vic couldn't believe his luck and was sure she had cured his Escort-driving lumbago.

Tonight, however, with her temper and his stubbornness, things could go spectacularly oblong.

He moved forward, put his arms round her waist and then cupped his hands round her breasts.

'Guess who?'

'The gasman.'

'I'll kill him.'

'You're early.'

'Yeah.' Then, trying to sound cool and casual about it, 'I finally quit the police department.'

Clanking the saucepan down, turning to face him. 'What?'

'Got myself a steady job.'

'Doing what?'

'I took the sleeper thing.'

Disentangling herself, moving away, swinging back round, chin tilted. 'I thought we were supposed to discuss it.'

'We are discussing it.'

'Don't try and bullshit me, Vic Hallam – every time I start to ask you about it, what it *entails*, what it *pays* – you start naffing on about bloody cottages with bloody roses rambling round the bloody door. For God's sake grow up man and start living in the real world like the rest of us sodding well have to –'

'The money's the same – more if you add on the exes –'

'Never mind the bloody exes – what are you going to do all bloody day long?'

'Same as I do now –'

'What – sit in the bloody boozer and then get shot at?'

'No,' trying to sound perfectly patient and reasonable, but also knowing it would irritate the shit out of her. 'There won't be any of that –'

'Oh no?'

'All I've got to do is keep my eyes and ears open –'

'For how bloody long?' Her voice becoming brusque and businesslike as if he were some pissed-up old dosser creating fuck in A&E reception: 'Come on Vic, how long is this so-called bloody job supposed to last?'

They were all the same, he thought. They were born knowing exactly how to go for the scrotum.

'Could be months, could be years –'

'Months – then what?' Leaning on the edge of the rickety paint-stained wallpapering table which was all they had left to eat off. 'Because if you think I'm bringing up this kiddie on a bloody copper's pension while you sit on your arse in a woolly hat with a bloody fishing rod in your hand singing Little Dolly bloody Daydream you can bloody well think again, my lad!'

That was Ellie all over: the more mad she got, the more Brummie she went – and not just Brummie, but old-fashioned fish-market Black Country Brummie. She must get it from her mother, he thought. Her mother had been born in Willenhall – 'Willenhall-where-the-locks-come-from', as Ellie always told him.

Any minute now she'd be calling him a 'gorby haddock'. It meant something between daft as a brush and thick as pigshit.

Vic grinned at her. It was a cop thing, grimed in by years of interviews over cigarette-end-scarred tables: the more somebody lost their rag, the more you encouraged it until finally they blew it and started digging their grave with their teeth.

'And you can take that bloody smile off your face!'

At that moment, confronted by her hot blue eyes and reddening neck, Vic saw it: the only way to win an argument with a woman – any woman.

He said, 'You're right.'

'Eh?'

15

'I said you're right. I must've been out my mind.'

'Why?' Not just frowning and suspicious now, but worried as well. 'Why? Come on Vic, what have you done?'

Laying on the seriousness. 'I'll tell you what I've done.'

'Go on, then.' Very quiet now.

Vic allowed himself a breath in, then out, and went on in a dull, even tone as though defeated by his own how-could-I-have-done-it stupidity: 'I saw Sam this morning. We talked about it. He nagged on and on. Finally I said I'd take the bloody job.' He looked up like a beaten dog. 'Anything to get out the Bridewell, away from arseholes like him and his greaseball sidekick Parnesy.' More defiantly, 'Anyway, I've arranged to go to the South Coast.'

'What?' He watched the emotions move across her face.

'I said I've arranged to go to the South Coast.'

'What about me?'

'I've got a lease on a house. For a year.'

'Where?'

'Place I told you about, St Bride's.'

'I thought we were going to get married first.'

'You still want to?'

'Don't you?'

'Yeah. Course.'

'When?'

'Soon as you like.' Time for a basic lie. 'I've been looking into it. Force gets preferential rates for either

16

the Mansion House or the *Great Britain*.' At least that bit was true –

Ellie said, 'Can my mother come?'

'Yeah. Course.'

Ellie thought for a moment. 'I don't think she'd manage all the steps on the *Great Britain*.'

Women and Boats –

'Fair enough. Mansion House it is then.'

She moved into his arms, kissed him, then sucked his tongue right in.

Even as he was pulling her pale blue uniform skirt up to get his hands on her magnificent backside he knew it was far too dangerous to mention the fifteen grand he'd just lobbed out on *Roy Roy*.

Following her into the bedroom, thinking what a dumb stupid prick-led bastard he was –

Then, afterwards, lying in his arms, she smiled contentedly up at him and said, 'You know, when you get going, Vic Hallam, you're a real man of decision, aren't you?'

'Well,' said Vic. 'Yes and no.'

3

A few weeks later, Vic bought the paper and took a post-breakfast walk along the quayside of St Bride's Harbour. It was a hot still early-May morning: high tide, dust on the water, reflections sliding underneath – and a tang of seaweed and mackerel-bait in the air: all the signs of a brilliant day and few, if any, tourists.

Great –

Vic tucked *The Times* under his arm, lit the first Marlboro of the day, and set out with the sun on his back thinking his luck had finally changed.

Twenty years of heavy drugs crime in Bristol getting thumped, carcrashed, stabbed once and shot twice, seeing good mates killed by crack-fuelled Yardies and murderous Turks – and now this:

He'd got married to Ellie; she was healthily pregnant, with no morning sickness; they were still on more or less permanent honeymoon, and she'd got a job lined up as a well-paid relief staff nurse at County Hospital starting in a couple of days' time. Even better, after Vic had moved the furniture around several times, she liked Flask Cottage, liked their neighbours, and was looking forward to her mother coming down for the end-of-May bank holiday.

Apart from that, Vic thought, he had a life in the sun, no bosses on his back, and his days his own for the first time in twenty years. Best of all – he had a half share in *Rob Roy*.

Taking it all round, it was a small price to pay for having his mother-in-law to the wedding. Ellie had gone very quiet when he'd told her he'd put fifteen grand into *Roy Roy*, but there hadn't been the flaming, plate-throwing row he expected.

Maybe they were different when they got married.

All she'd done, after going to see Joe's wife Cathy, a rangy blonde woman in her thirties with whom she'd struck up an instant but clearly necessary female alliance, was to insist that Vic put the remaining forty-five grand from the sale of the flat into a building-society joint account where she could see what was happening to it. Cathy had told her you had to agree on three things for a good marriage: food, sex and money. You had to be there to feed the brute, you had to have sex after rows, and you had to have a joint account.

Vic said, 'Is that it?'

'That's the deal.'

'Can't we have a row about it?'

'Don't you think about anything else?'

'Course I do.'

'Such as?'

'Fishing. Supposed to be some early spider crab about.'

That was the point, according to Ellie: at least she'd

know where he was, he wouldn't be all day in the pub, they'd always have plenty of fresh fish, which was good for pregnant women, and once the season got going after Whitsun the charter money from the holiday anglers would come in handy.

Vic was so relieved at getting away with his half share in *Rob Roy* he even went shopping for flat-pack bedroom furniture in Bournemouth with her –

Coming out of his reverie, Vic flicked away the half-smoked Marlboro and heard it fizz in the water. A herring gull scythed down on it, one wingtip millimetres from the surface, clocked the sodden dog-end for what it was, banked and soared up again, levelled, hung in the air, then sideslipped up and away into the blue.

Beautiful things, seagulls – apart from the fact they splattered crap over everything –

Vic looked out across the harbour, filled his chest with fresh salty air, shoved his hands in the bottom pockets of his padded tartan shirt, and walked on with a rare smile on his face.

Where had it all gone right, Hallam?

Even more to the point, how could it all go wrong?

Ka-doink – ka-doink . . .

The, getting faster, madder:

Ka-doink-ka-doink-ka-doink!

Metal on metal reverberating out across the stone-walled nineteenth-century harbour and back again. Vic reached the timbered knuckle where the Inner

Harbour met the Cut leading to the newly built Outer Harbour, and looked over the side.

Crouched on the open rear deck of *Rob Roy* his fishing partner Joe Moore, heavily built, dark-haired and grizzle-bearded, was laying into the innards of a second-hand 60hp Mercury outboard with a twelve-pound lump-hammer. Vic recognised the engine from the black engine-cover lying upturned on the deck: he and Joe had bought it the weekend before. Now Vic watched three hundred and fifty quid being pounded into scrap.

Joe worked away at its destruction in concentrated silence. He looked neither out of breath nor angry. Bits of bright alloy cooling fin flew through the air from each bare-armed thick-wristed blow.

'Morning, Joe.'

Joe glanced up and squinted against the sun. 'Morning, Vic.' He didn't sound particularly stressed, but then he never did: the only signs of anger were the tell-tale red marks under his eyes.

Then Joe went back to work, one massive black-haired hand holding the chromed shaft steady while the other, clenched round the lump-hammer, battered remorselessly away at the finned cylinder head. More bits of alloy flew. Vic sat on a rounded anvil-shaped cast-iron bollard and watched.

The two men were of an age, give or take a month or so, and in the thirty-odd years they had known each other, Vic had witnessed his friend's rage erupting no more than half a dozen times. Joe never took it out on people or animals, not even on homicidal villains or big blue-black congers whose ridged bite could go through leather and flesh to the bone beneath, but always on mechanical things and usually with a hammer, or an iron bar if there was no hammer handy.

Vic had once seen Joe smash the jammed fifteen-inch iron roller of a pot-haul winch in two with one blow; there was no point in trying to talk to him – once he was off, he was off.

Afterwards he was right as rain: no excuses, no apologies, no sheepishness; just the same big, calm, slow-moving, heavy-limbed Joe Vic had always known.

The first time Vic had seen it happen was back in Bristol in the early seventies. They were eight years old, and for the previous two days they had been playing a complicated battle game of lead soldiers in Joe's back garden. They had fixed positions, defiles, machine-gun posts, redoubts with matchstick-firing cannon, and about two hundred lead soldiers, all Joe's, infantry and cavalry representing every period from the Boer War to World War Two. The game was played according to the strict and increasingly elaborate rules of engagement they had worked out between them, and involved a set of Crown and Anchor dice Joe's soldier-father had brought back from abroad. Joe's father had told him the yellowing round-edged cubes were whalebone and made by sailors on the whaling ships. They were heavy and cool in the hand; to their boyish imaginations the five worn pieces were full of luck and magic.

When Vic had arrived for the third morning, he found the front curtains closed. Joe let him in and said quietly his mum was upstairs. On the mantelpiece in front of the ivory-faced seven-day Smiths' clock was a fawn telegram obscuring the hands. Out in the garden Joe looked at the lines and clusters of painted lead soldiers and said he didn't want to play any more because it would upset his mother. Together they picked up all the soldiers and put them back flat in their dark green wooden ammunition box. Then Joe led Vic down to the bottom of the garden out through a gap in the paling fence to the waste ground beyond.

He got Vic to light a fire from scrap cardboard, grass, twigs and pieces of rotten fence-wood while he smashed the soldiers up inside the wooden ammo box with half a housebrick. When the fire was red-hot Joe piled on more fence-wood in layers, building up a small square pyre. Then he poured a medicine bottle of blue paraffin into the box, closed the lid, laid it on the fire and stood quickly back. For a second or two thick blue smoke plumed out of the box and then the lid blew open. Inside, the bent, mangled figures of the lead soldiers melted and swam in a sea of orange fire and bluish flame.

'Good, eh?' said Joe, the skin below his eyes reddened, a fixed grin daring Vic to contradict him. 'It's good, innit?'

'Yeah,' said Vic. 'Great.'

They watched in hot-faced silence until the ammo box blackened and crumbled. Joe raked the unburnt wood base out with a stick. Inside there was an irregular lake of silver that misted over and dimmed even as they watched. When it was solid enough, Joe fished it out on to the grass, folded it over like a pancake and bashed it with the housebrick until it was a dull lead block. Then he carried it down to the brick-filled pool at the bottom of the waste ground and threw it in. He watched the ripples for a while, then turned to Vic and said, 'I got to go in now. Mum's not well.'

When Vic got home his mother took him aside and told him that Joe's father had been killed by a sniper in Belfast.

4

'Feeling better now?'

Joe stopped hammering and glowered up at Vic. 'You always were a sarcastic bastard, you know that?'

Vic shrugged. 'Goes with the job.'

'Yeah, I remember.'

'And half that three hundred and fifty quid was mine.'

Joe held out the lump-hammer. 'You want a go?'

'Just wondering why, that's all.'

'Last fucking straw, mate.'

'How come?'

'Bank's still playing fuck over the house. Had a letter this morning saying they want to put a surveyor in, check out the place is worth as much as I say it is.' Joe took a sheet of headed A4 parchment out of his top pocket. 'Otherwise they're still threatening foreclosure, repossession and taking me to court for fraud and possible theft on the basis of "supplying misleading information with regard to fraudulently obtaining a loan".' He put the letter back and buttoned down his top pocket. 'Fucking banks. One minute they're falling over themselves to give you the money, the next they bite your fucking arm off –'

'Have they got a case?'

'I don't fucking know.' Joe looked over at the Old Customs House across the harbour. It had been a derelict shell with a corrugated iron roof and breeze-blocked windows when Joe and Cath bought it; now it was a handsome porticoed building painstakingly restored to its late-Georgian origins, right down to the slated octagonal watchtower on the roof. 'Took five years of my bastard life to do that place up, all the original plans and materials, even the right shades of fucking paint, all the time Cath and me and the kids living in a fucking Portakabin in the middle of it all – and now they want to send some snooty-arsed fucker in to look at the walls, the wiring, the fucking roof, all the fucking bills and specs. Well there are no fucking bills and specs. I did it all. More cunt me.' He tossed the lump-hammer into the remains of the outboard and looked up at Vic like a beaten dog. 'Cath's going berserk. Got a fag?'

Vic threw the pack of Marlboro on to the deck. 'How much they want? I mean, how much to hold 'em off – anything I can do?'

'Thanks all the same but they don't mention that. This surveyor bloke sends in the sort of report they want, they've got the house and the boat. That's how it looks anyway. Sorry mate.'

Vic said nothing.

'Anyway I come down here, strap this thing on the stern, start her up, give her a few revs – ten seconds later the drive's stripped and the fucking shaft's cracked.

Look at this.' Joe swivelled the propeller to and fro: it made a clacking noise. 'Fucking thing's knackered.'

'It is now.'

Joe grinned despite himself, and heaved the hundredweight of battered engine one-handed on to the quay. 'Knackered and they knew it. Least they won't sell the bastard to any other fucker.' He swung himself up on to the cockpit coming and stepped ashore. 'What a fucking day –'

Vic said, 'Seemed all right when we tried it in their water tank.' The marine surveyor had told them new safety regulations required a more powerful auxiliary and Joe had reckoned the 60hp Mercury was strong enough to push *Rob Roy* home if the main screws got fouled.

'Nothing to drive against in a tank.' Joe hoisted the outboard motor on to his shoulder. 'Can you get the engine cover?'

'Sure. Where we going?'

'Get our money back. I reckon somebody's spot-welded the bloody thing and bodged the fucker up to sell.'

Vic followed Joe round the Old Harbour over the bridge and sluice-gates and up to the Cut to the new deep-water all-weather quay where the big offshore fishing boats were moored.

The old Portland-stone Harbour Master's Office had been demolished and a new breezeblock Chandlery and Fishery Supplies Depot built along-side equally new fish-marketing and cold-storage units. As soon as he stepped out on to the new Sea Wall, Vic felt the sea breeze: the air temperature dropped five degrees or so.

Visibility was still diamond-clear, and Vic could see the full length of his patch, and far beyond: way off to the south-west lay a low grey line of headlands fingering out to Start Point some sixty miles away. Beyond that lay nothing but the Atlantic until you came to the West Indies. Nearer home came the whitish cliffs around Seaton and Beer Head; the landslips of rotten clay lias around Lyme; the bright, sand-topped bar of Golden Cap, then more crumbling blue lias cliffs as you closed St Bride's. Off to the east lay the long curve of the Chesil Bank, twenty-two miles of uninterrupted sand-and-shingle beach. The Chesil, as the locals called it, rose to the quarry-scarred hump of Portland Bill and terminated in its single stark white light.

From Exmouth in the west to Poole in the east, a hundred miles of cliff and beach had been recently designated a UNESCO World Heritage Site, and dubbed, as much for tourist purposes as the chance of finding any decent fossils, 'The Jurassic Coast'.

A lee shore in the prevailing westerlies, the long curve between St Bride's and Portland had proved fatal to scores of stormbound squareriggers unable to round the Bill against the south-westerly gales. Driven on to the Chesil, dozens of ships and cargoes had gone down, hundreds of sailors had drowned, and for years the sea area west of Portland had been known as

'Dead Man's Bay'. Even now the scouring action of the tidal currents on the constantly shifting gravel bottom threw up new wrecks every year.

'Not that you'd know,' Joe had told him, 'these charter fishermen are cunning old buggers. They find a new wreck, they keep it to themselves. None of 'em leave their charts on their boats. You'll see 'em staggering off home at night, they might be three parts pissed but they've still got their charts rolled up under their arm like a bunch of geriatric fucking admirals.'

'Why's that then?'

'Money, Vic. All most of these buggers are interested in. You find a new wreck, it's as good as money in the bank. You'll get a deckload of divers all season long, and after that you got wreck-fishing through the winter. Conger, pollack, ling, even bass, they all love a wreck. Somewhere to lie low in, keep their heads down and wait for the next meal to come swimming along. Makes a good mark for the sort of business you're interested in.'

'You mean a boat could home in on a wreck, drop off a load of smack or whatever for some other bugger to pick up later?'

'Yeah, easy.'

'How?'

'You get one of these hand-held satnavs, call up the courier boat on your mobile, dial in their coordinates for the wreck where they've dropped off the load, and you can drive down to the beach, get your swimmers on – your hand-held satnav will put you within six feet of it.'

'Handy.'

'Moonless night, any kid in a scuba suit can make a pick-up off the drop location and walk ashore with a million quid's worth of H in a plastic sack, dump it in a Land-Rover, up and away and nobody any the wiser.'

'Why a Land-Rover?'

Joe grinned. 'We've all been on traffic, Vic. You ever stopped anybody in a Land-Rover?'

'Not that I recall –'

'Me neither. They're slow, they're agricultural, nobody in their right mind would use one for a getaway car. But in the country – specially round here – they're invisible, indestructible and they run on cheap pink diesel. You can be pissed as a fart and you'll never get stopped in one. Why all the crafty old buggers round here use 'em.'

When they reached the Chandlery, Joe unshouldered the Mercury and held out his hand for the engine cover. 'I'll deal with this, Vic.'

'You're not anticipating anything physical, are you?'

'Not with the prats that work here.'

To pass the time, Vic walked out along the new £17 million breakwater to look at the big bluff-ended commercial fishing vessels. There were half a dozen, ranging from 45 to 60 feet, registered from South

Coast locations as far apart as Newlyn and Newhaven.

Vic was idly checking out the two-letter port codes painted on their bows when his mobile beeped: Bristol Central CID.

Here we go again, Hallam –

Reluctantly he pressed the YES key.

5

A female voice said, 'DS Hallam?'

'Yeah?'

'Can you speak?'

'Speaking now, aren't I?'

'Chief Superintendent Richardson for you.'

'Morning Sam.'

'Morning Vic. What's the weather like?'

'Brilliant –'

'Pissing down here in Bristol.'

'Sorry to hear that, Sam.'

'No you're not, so put your fucking fishing rod down and get yourself over to Portland, *now*. Got your ID on you?'

'No –'

'Well go home and get it. I don't care what you're doing, just drop everything and get over there. We could have first touch on this Kingfisher thing –'

'Right –'

'What's that fucking row for Christ sake?'

Vic looked over at the nearest fishing boat. One of the crew was chucking a bucket of shiny red slime over the stern and about fifty herring gulls were screaming down, pecking and fighting over the fish guts. It was all over in seconds: most of the stuff was gone before it hit the water.

Vic said, 'Seagulls, Sam.'

'Fucking Christ –'

'Where d'you want me to go, Sam?'

'What – oh – you know HMP *Aware*?'

'The prison ship, was the old *Resolve*?'

'Yeah, that's the one. Give me your car reg. and I'll tell 'em you're coming –'

'And when I get there?'

'You're a ward orderly.' Vic heard a rustle of paper. 'You're in what they call "sickbay" and you're looking after a kiddy called Dutchy or Doochy or some such daft fucking name. A black kid anyway –'

'Got it. What's he in for?'

'Was a coke dealer and fixer operating as middleman between the Colombians and the Yardie posses. Got picked up for an ounce of hash in Avonmouth and sent down the Verne with the rest of our black friends. Anyway this guy speaks the Colombians' fucking lingo, knows all the concealment dodges, travels with the stuff, fixes up the drop zones and handovers but neither mob lets him touch the money. They don't trust any fucker unless they've got a gun on him. Mostly that's how he's kept out of trouble over here. The Yanks have got warrants out but we've got the man himself. Now he's had the shit beaten out of him.'

'Who by?'

'Bunch of Balkanians.' It was what Sam called all

refugees: Kurds, Slavs, Afghanis, the lot. 'All picked up for illegal entry but all of 'em known to run hookers and smack. Now they're sitting on their arses at our expense waiting for their so-called fucking families to pick up a free house and hundreds of quid a week in benefits. What a fucking country, Vic, they come over here to rip us off and then they claim fucking asylum – you ask me, asylum's the right place for most of the dirty-arse thieving fuckpigs –'

'Yes, Sam.' Sam, as Vic knew, was a *Daily Mail* reader.

'Anyway this Doochy kid's pretty bad apparently, so you better get over there and see what he's got to say. State he's in he may well want to cough some fucking deal or other and drop somebody else in the shit – probably these fucking Balkanians –'

'You say these guys are into smack?'

'That and everything else they can lay their fucking hands on.'

'What's smack got to do with crack? I mean if he's a coke dealer that's his dap-off, that's his trade. These guys don't mix it – it's too fucking dangerous. Neither mob wants the other butting in, taking over. Even the Yardies have to buy smack in before they can run it –'

'Up to you to find out. I'm not here to wipe your arse for you.'

'Thanks, Sam.'

'My pleasure.'

*

Ellie was spray-starching and ironing her uniforms when Vic got back to Flask Cottage. 'Hear you coming a mile off, crunching over that gravel.'

'That's what it's there for.' Vic had laid a couple of inches of pea gravel over the flagstone path to the front door. He'd also fitted window bolts, intruder lights, hardened steel drop-chains and bull's-eye inspection glasses on both front and back doors. Ellie had watched but said nothing. Vic told her it was better to be safe than sorry, you got all sorts of fly-by-nights and door-knocker-wrenchers hanging round holiday homes on the lookout for something to nick.

Ellie had still said nothing.

Now she said, 'You're back early.'

Vic was already halfway up the narrow open staircase between the sitting room and the kitchen. 'I've got to go to Portland.' He came back down stuffing boxer shorts and shaving things into a Nike sportsbag.

Ellie looked at him. 'It's started, hasn't it?'

'Could say that.' He searched his jacket pockets for the keys to the Vauxhall Cavalier Diesel.

'How long for?'

'A day, two, not much longer. I've got to talk to a bloke in HMP *Aware*.'

'What's HMP *Aware* when it's out?'

'It's the prison ship, the hulk where they keep the prisoners due for release away from the Verne main prison.'

'I see.'

35

Vic took his ID out of his wallet and stuck it in his shirt pocket. 'What's a ward orderly do?'

'As little as possible most of the time. Why?'

'It's what I'm supposed to be.'

'You make beds, mop the floor, help them eat their food, clean up sick and take the bedridden to the baths and bogs.'

'Sounds fascinating.'

'Vic – if I'm not here when you get back –'

His mind raced and his speech slowed down. 'If you're not here, when I get back – what?'

'I shall be at work. I start the County Hospital job day after tomorrow.'

'Oh yeah. Well –' He glanced at his watch. 'Look love, I got to go. I'll get the hospital number. D'you know which ward you'll be on?'

'Not yet, no.'

They stood facing each other. When Vic put his arms round her, sportsbag still in hand, it took a couple of moments for her to unstiffen and let him kiss her. 'Well, good luck, love.'

'Thanks.'

'I'll give you a call when I know what's happening –'

Now she was clinging to him. 'Vic –'

'What?'

'Be careful.'

'Yeah, I will.' He kissed her again then pulled himself away. 'Good luck again with the job if I don't see you before.'

Ellie stood in the small sitting room listening to his feet crunching rapidly away from her over the gravel. She heard the wicket gate clack open and shut, then she picked up the steam-iron and frowned at its perforated aluminium base as if she had forgotten what it was for.

Vic took the coast road to Weymouth and Portland. Even in the ten-year-old Cavalier Diesel the B3157 was one of the best driving roads he knew, and where it opened up after Burton Bradstock and began to swoop up and down over open heathland with the great blinding blue shield of the sea far below to the right, it was a roller-coaster of sheer exhilaration. Even now, he thought, no matter how grubby the job or how boring the daily bloody grind, all it took was something like this, something as simple as sea, grass, sky and an open road, to pick up your heart and send it skimming and soaring free from all the work-and-money-worry rat-hounds clicking their steel teeth round your testicles . . .

Better than being stuck in sticky-arsed Central Bristol traffic all day long.

He came over the top and down the steep LOW GEAR NOW slope into Abbotsbury. In front of him, St Catherine's Tower on its cone-shaped hill, beyond that the narrow gleam of the saltwater Fleet, and off to the right of the dark green diamond-shape of the Subtropical Gardens.

He remembered going there with Ellie on a damp

April day and how saucer-eyed and sensually drugged she became as they wandered through the massed heavily scented magnolias, the towering ferns and ragged palms: there was a musky wet-earth fragrance somewhere between mushrooms and chestnut that hung like mist in the air between the shiny deep green leaves.

'You know what that smell reminds me of, Vic?'

'What?'

'Fresh come.' She glanced round to see if they were alone and pulled him close up against her. Then she whispered, 'Do it to me, Vic. Push me down and do it to me.'

So he did. He took her through the rain-soaked bushes, and laid her down on a patch of dry ground underneath a low-branched conifer. She pulled her knickers to one side. 'Now Vic, now.'

Her fingers dug deep into the loose pine-needled soil.

Afterwards, they walked back arm in arm to the car just like any other normal married couple.

Vic wondered how well you can ever know another human being.

All the same, he went into the gift shop and bought her the deepest red-black rose he could find.

Going through the stop-and-start traffic on the outskirts of Weymouth Vic called Joe, told him about Portland and asked whether he'd got the money back on the Mercury outboard. Joe said the toerags didn't have that much in the till and anyway he'd have to speak to the boss.

'Who's the boss?'

'He's never there. Name of Giffen. Also known as Scrump.'

'Big bad-tempered guy looks as if he's got it on him?'

'That's him. Bit of a dealer. Does the white-van run across the Channel. Fags, booze, food – anything that's cheaper over there '

'Second-hand outboards?'

'All right, I know –'

'Any form?'

'Affray, assault, going equipped. Banned from all the pubs in the harbour so he gets on the scrump up the town.'

'Watch it, Joe.'

'Got more than him to worry about mate.'

6

HMP *Aware*, shorn of *Resolve*'s guns, painted grey drab
and chained to the bottom, looked as much a prisoner
as the poor buggers it contained. On board it smelt
like an old Channel ferry, a queasy mixture of diesel,
cooking oil, ammoniac toilets, disinfectant and a faint
cabbage-fart odour of long-lying bilge-water. Below
decks there was a hum of generators, ventilators – and
another, added smell: stale male sweat.

After Vic had been issued with a high-collared
jacket, thick black serge trousers and a heavy bunch
of keys on a steel chain, a prison officer led him along
a clanging metalled passageway to the sickbay
amidships.

'Doochy's the only one in there. He's still under
sedation so he won't be much trouble. If he needs
attention, ring for it.'

'Right.'

'Best of luck, then.' The officer slapped Vic on the
shoulder, and grinned. 'Only thing is, don't let him
bite you.'

'Why, what is he, a vampire?'

'Worse than that.'

Doochy was lying on top of his bunk in a white op

gown that failed to reach his knees. His eyes were closed and his body had the wasted look of a Somali famine victim: thin arms and legs bandaged round the joints, shrivelled greyish skin where muscles used to be; a skull-like head, bruised and bandaged, with hollow temples and sunken eye-sockets; dry lips drawn back over a grin of ivory-yellow teeth.

He looked at least fifty; his notes, slotted at the foot of his bunk in a plastic holder, told Vic he was twenty-six years old; his full name was Julian Duchene; he was born in Castries, St Lucia; by profession he was a merchant seaman but also had an extant criminal record as a drug courier; and that he was in sickbay for observation and treatment of multiple contusions sustained in an assault. At the foot of the notes, someone had written in thick red Pentel: HIV+

'Only thing is, don't let him bite you.'

Doochy's eyes opened. 'Hi man. Who a fuck a you?'

'I'm Victor Thompson, Julian, relief ward orderly.'

'Ain' no relief to me, man.'

'Do you have any pain, Julian?' It was what nurses asked.

'Doochy – like ever'body else –' His voice faded and his eyes closed. Without opening them, he whispered, 'You a cop, man. You walk like a cop. Doochy hear you comin', and you walk like a cop. So fuck off, cop, you hear me nah?'

It was all he said until the lunch trolley clattered

along the metalled walkway. Vic opened the door and took the insulated plastic tray.

'Lunchtime Doochy.'

'Help me up, man.'

Vic propped up the headrest and hauled Doochy up from behind, careful to keep his head and hands away from Doochy's face. The poor kid was as light and dry as a bundle of twigs.

'What we got?'

Vic lifted up the heat-retaining cover. In one indent of the tray was a piece of grey skinless fish and a small flat-topped mound of rice. In the other was a thick tongue of yellow custard with a sliver of red jelly on top. Doochy ate the rice and the jelly and pushed the tray slowly and deliberately on to the floor.

'Is all shit man. Is all white shit.'

'Couldn't agree more,' said Vic, and started to clean it up.

'Heh heh heh,' said Doochy, and lay back and went to sleep.

Doochy slept all afternoon, breathing through his mouth and making small grunty throat-clearing noises.

In the humming silence Vic thought he had never felt so alone, cooped up and cut off from ordinary fresh-air reality in his whole life. How did people do these fucking jobs? And why?

At six, when the light had faded from the barred east-facing wire-mesh grille, the food trolley came clanking round. This time it was kedgeree with jam and semolina. Doochy ate half of each pile and tried to push the tray off again. This time Vic was ready for him and took the tray out of his resistless grey hands.

'Heh heh heh.'

Vic's supper was from half past six to seven. Goulash, dark brown tea and a mandarin orange. He took it in the messroom during the change-over when the night staff accompanied the drug trolley round. When he came back for his last three-hour stint Doochy was sitting up in his bunk smoking a big six-skin joint.

'What the fuck –'

'This place, you gotta have a stash, man.'

'Yeah but –' Vic stopped himself: it could be the break he was looking for. All he said was. 'You got a fucking nerve, Doochy.'

'Heh heh heh. What you gonna do, *Victa* – bus' me?' With a lazy wave he offered Vic the wet-ended joint.

'No thanks, Doochy.'

'Local grass, man. The screws grow it an' bring it in. You wanna keep the guys quiet and boost you money up, thass what you do.' Again he waved the joint at Vic. 'Come on man, ain't gonna kill ya.'

'Tell you the truth, I don't go a lot on it –'

Doochy suddenly sat up, leaning forward, dark eyes blazing, yellow teeth spitting out the words like bullets. 'No man, *I* tell you the fuckin' truth – what you don't go a lot on is *Haids* – ain' I right? Ain' Doochy right? Ain' that the truth? Ain' that what you scared of? Ol' Doochy gonna suck his gums an' spit blood in you eye an' you gonna be *hin-fected –*' He spat, Caribbean-style, through his front teeth. Vic recoiled, looked down at the stain on his white jacket. Dark rusty brown.

'You bastard –'

'Heh heh heh. You dumb white piece of shit.'

Vic wiped off the stain with a wodge of wet tissue. 'I'm sorry, Doochy –'

'What you mean, *you* fuckin' sorry?'

'I shouldn't have said that.'

Doochy leaned back, took a long pull at the joint, held it in, eyes closed, then slowly and luxuriously blew it out. 'Ain' *you* who is sorry man, is *me* who is sorry.'

'Yeah.' Vic scraped the sole grey plastic chair closer to Doochy's bunk until there was only a foot or so between them.

'You tryin' to show me you ain' scared?'

'Partly.'

'An' what else?'

'How d'you come to get in this mess?'

'Which mess that, man? The Haids mess or the beat-up mess?'

'Whichever.'

'Long story, man.'

'We got the time.'

'Yeah, ain't we.' Doochy took another drag, looked beyond Vic into the distance, into the past. It was so long before he spoke Vic thought he'd lost him, that he was drifting off to sleep again. Then: 'I got Haids in Durban. Off the black girls . . . big, fine-looking black girls. Zulu kids. Got a shine on 'em like a heggplant. Ass like a rock an' a mouth like a big black plum. Yeah . . .' He shook his head sadly. 'But they all got Haids, man – why their fam'lies send 'em down to work the dockside.'

'You in the Merch?'

'Yeah.'

'My old man was. On the Fyffes boats. Picking up all the way down from Jamaica to Barbados. He loved it down there.'

Doochy cocked his head and grinned. 'Them Bajans ain't worth a fuck, man. Nor them Yardie boys. He ever call in St Lucia?'

Vic decided it was worth the lie to keep him talking: 'Said it was the Jewel of the Caribbean.'

'Ain' it a fack?' Grinning broadly now. 'May soun' like bullshit, but it's true, man.' He bit off the soggy end of the joint, looked slyly at Vic, then spat it on the floor. Vic pulled out his battered Imco lighter and relit the joint. 'Thanks, man. You know what?'

'What?'

He looked at Vic frankly. His eyes starting to glisten. 'I don' wanna die here, man. Not in this cold damn frien'less countree. When I go I wanta feel the sun on my bones.'

Maybe that was an angle –

'Where else have you been, Doochy?'

It turned out he had gone to sea at fourteen, spent

a few years on illegal whalers out of Durban ploughing deep into the South Atlantic but making good money off the Japs, going home, getting married, then gambling everything away in St Lucia, leaving his wife and kids to try and make out with the Jamaicans in New York, getting busted, in and out of bad deals, bad women, bad jails . . . 'I been on an' off every fuckin' piece a junk that floats, from rotted-out Mexican tramps to stinkin' Nigerian oil-tankers . . . I sailed outa every kind of bug-ridden shithole port from Galveston to Yokohama, Sydney in Australia up to Anchorage in Alaska . . . All in all I reckon I spent more time at sea than I ever done ashore. All that sea-time, man, an' I ain' never got back to St Lucia not once . . . Got nothin' to show for it but the wors' fuckin' disease in the world an' then I end up in here, beat up to fuck in the wors' fuckin' ship I ever been on. Holy shit —'

'How d'you get beat up?'

'Bunch a guys done it for not tellin' them what I ain't tellin' you.'

'Fair enough.'

Doochy leaned forward. 'You ever made any real money, Victa?'

'Not a lot.'

'Me neither. But now I got a chance I ain' tellin' no fucker. Seen?'

'Yeah, seen.'

Doochy put the joint between his thumb and third finger and sucked out the last drag. His red-rimmed eyelids began to droop. Now was the time.

Lose him now, Hallam, and you lose him for ever —

'What do you most want, Doochy?'

'Wha'?'

'You had the choice, what's the thing you most want in all the world?'

'In all the world?' Doochy looked up, the taut skin on his face creasing in concentration, his chin on the steeple of his knuckles, the half-moons of his finger-nails almond-pale against the bony jut of his jaw. Yet again Vic thought he had lost him. Then his voice came, hoarse, desolate, no more than a whisper: 'I wanna go home, Victa – I wanna go home.'

7

In the morning, as a result of his phone call to Ellie and what she had told him of the relationship between HIV and Aids, Vic rang Sam Richardson.

'He talk?'

'Not a lot,' said Vic. 'Not so far.'

'Why the fuck not? You've had all day with him – I thought you were supposed to be good at breaking people down?'

'The kid's medicated up to the eyeballs.'

'So?'

'He sleeps all day.'

'Can't you get 'em to take him off it?'

'Not after the going-over he's had. These guys had two-foot lengths of inch-insulated cable. They laid into him all over. Head, arms, legs, every joint in his fucking body. Not to mention his bollocks. They knew what they were doing, Sam.'

'Meaning what?'

'If they wanted to kill him they would have, no problem. They had him to themselves, locked in the showers for twenty minutes before anybody could get to him.'

'And he still wouldn't tell 'em?'

'Wouldn't tell me either.'

Silence as Sam chewed it over. Then, coming to a decision: 'So. Either somebody's put serious frighteners on him – somebody else, I mean, not these half-baked Balkanians – or there's something in it for himself. When's he due out?'

'Was going to be next week or so – you only get end-of-sentence guys on the *Aware*. State he's in now, it's hard to tell.'

'Why's that, Vic?'

'Kid's a bundle of bones . . . Come on, Sam – you knew he was HIV positive.'

A brief silence, then Sam snorted a dismissive laugh.

Vic felt like slamming the phone down. He controlled himself, and waited.

'I didn't want to worry you, Vic.'

'Thanks a bunch.'

'No hard feelings, I hope.'

Cunt –

'You still there, Vic?'

'Yeah, I'm here.'

'So what d'you reckon?'

'Well. He did ask me if I'd ever made any real money.'

'And you said?'

'Not a lot.'

'Then what? Come on, Vic – he make you a deal, offer to cut you in?'

'No such luck –'

'For Christ sake, Hallam – like trying to get blood out of a stone –'

'All he said was now he had the chance he wasn't going to tell no fucker – including me.'

'Fuckhead's playing silly buggers –'

'You haven't seen him, Sam. What he's been through and still kept schtum, all he was telling me was I got no chance of getting anything –'

'Fucking Balkanians didn't beat the shit out of him for nothing, Vic –'

'All right. Suppose he is in on some kind of deal, drop or whatever. That's what he specialises in, but now he thinks he's on the money. It's got to be with one of the posses because that's all he knows. On the other hand he doesn't go a lot on the Yardies so maybe it's direct with the Colombians. But they don't like operating over here, so everywhere you turn it's one brick wall after another. All we know is that these guys on the *Aware* knew something about something and tried to beat it out of him –'

'There you are. I was right –'

'They failed, Sam. Back to square one. We all are.'

'Look Vic, all we need to know is where and when –'

'Yeah.'

'Got to be a way.'

'Yeah.'

'I'm relying on you, Vic.' A pause to see if the soft-soap was working. 'Any ideas?' Another pause. 'Anything at all, Vic?'

'The kid thinks he's dying, Sam.'

'Well, he's right there, isn't he?'

'He wants to go home. Back to St Lucia. He said when he goes he wants to feel the sun on his bones.'

Another brief snort. 'His hard fucking luck –'

'No it isn't, Sam, it's the only fucking lever we've got.'

'Talking about?'

'I think he means it. He's got a wife and kids over there.'

'Oh come on, Vic, they got wives and kids everywhere.'

Vic knew he was very close to the end of his patience. 'All I'm saying is you should have seen him. HIV or no, he's a real fucking hard nut, he's roughed it all over, been in every kind of fucking jail from arsehole to breakfast time. He got me sussed for a copper straight away. I was nowhere near cracking him till I asked him what he really wanted. He said "I wanna go home". His eyes were watering, Sam –'

'Yeah yeah yeah –'

'For Christ sake Sam!' Shouting now. 'I got to have something to offer the poor bastard!'

Silence, then: 'You're going soft, Hallam. Soft in the fucking head –'

'You want me to do this fucking job or not?'

'Temper temper –'

'Listen then –'

'. . . I'm listening, Vic.'

'What I want to do is offer to put this guy on a

Protected Witness Programme and fly him back to a safe house in St Lucia.'

'Vic, Vic – he's not big enough. 'Part from anything else, the poor black cunt's got Aids.'

'No he hasn't, Sam, he thinks he has, just like you do.'

'Talking in fucking riddles now.'

'If he's in the middle on this one, he's big enough. And there's a difference between HIV and having Aids full blown.'

'Such as?'

'One you can treat. One you can't.' It wasn't as simple as that, but what the fuck, what did Sam know?

'Where d'you get this from?'

'Ellie.'

'Oh yeah. Trust me I'm a nurse.'

'That's right, Sam.'

One more fucking word . . .

But Sam, as usual, knew when to back off. 'So. In return for some pissy little chance of Information Received you want me to set up a deal, and a fucking expensive deal at that?'

'All I'm saying is, talk to the guys in SO22, talk to the Chief Commissioner out there, Superintendent or whoever he is, tell 'em all we think we've got the piggy in the middle, see which way the wind blows –'

'Vic.'

'I'm not going to con anything out of him, Sam. Kid's too fly.'

'All right. Don't do anything till I call you back.'
The line went dead.

Vic smoked three Marlboros over breakfast in the messroom trying to get his head sorted over Doochy and how much, in the light of what Ellie had said, he ought to tell the kid.

Ellie rarely talked about her work, not about the important stuff anyway: you were supposed to save life and alleviate suffering, but sometimes the two met in a head-on collision and how the fuck did you decide what to do then? It was all too much like life-and-death on a daily basis, and how the fuck did you make chit-chat out of that? It was something that Ellie, like most nurses in Vic's experience, preferred to leave in the ward, or, more likely, keep to themselves; then go out and get shagged brainless on Chardonnay.

It was the same thing for coppers: you didn't traipse a load of death and disaster home on your boots, you stayed out and got pissed and forgot about it. Because if you didn't you'd go mad –

But this time she had soberly and comprehensively laid it on him; told him, in effect, what his responsibilities were.

She said treatment for long-term HIV-positives in Doochy's category could be not only unreliable but hugely expensive: 'Outside a controlled environment like a ward, Vic, or isolation such as you say he's in now, all kinds of things can happen. Stress, accident, a family row. Not to mention the kind of diseases we don't have over here that are endemic over there –'

'Endemic in what sense?'

'In the water, the air, sanitation, food preparation, other people.'

'Holy shit.'

'He could easily end up being not just a danger to himself, but life-threatening to anybody he comes in contact with.'

'Yeah, I hadn't thought of that –'

'Well you should have.'

'Yes, nurse.'

'It's not funny, Victor.'

'No, I know.'

'I just don't know whether they've got the money or the facilities, Vic. Neither do you. And until you do, nobody in any position of medical responsibility would dare make a decision that could leave the patient incapacitated and his lawyers suing. You're not in that position, Vic. It's not up to you.'

Then, quietly and firmly, she'd put the phone down.

He'd already decided there was no point in telling Sam: so long as he got the information he wanted, Doochy could get fucked all ends up and all Sam would do was laugh.

But what about Doochy?

Was there a deal or was the kid deluding himself?

Knowing he was on his last legs, telling himself he'd walk out a winner?

A lot of crims did that: defiant to the fucking last –

In any case what should Vic tell him?

That even if he was going home, it was in all probability to die?

The poor kid thought that anyway.

But suppose he, Vic, was sending home a walking time-bomb?

Well, bedridden anyway –

Fucking hell, Hullam, what have you done?

Vic stubbed out his cigarette and stood up hoping that Sam would get the thumbs-down from the higher-ups. Then nothing would happen and life would go on as normal, or at least what passed for normal in this humming airless fucking hellhole, and he could get out and leave the whole poxy business behind.

Unlike poor old Doochy.

Well, shit happens.

Trouble was, you could figure the odds any way you liked, and you could still never tell which sort of shit was going to happen.

Only that it was the sort you hadn't bargained for.

8

'How you doing, Doochy?' Five minutes past ten and Doochy had already had a bed bath and his dressings changed.

'I jus' seen my balls, Victa. They all swole up black an' green like a coupla halligator pears, an' I'm still pissin' blood. Apart from that everythin' fine, man. Heh heh heh.'

'You got guts, kid.'

'Yeah . . . You seen anythin' a them dirty-ass rass done all this?'

'They're in solitary. I had a look at their statements.'

The prison officer who made out the internal inquiry reports had told Vic they all claimed not to speak English and when they asked to get another prisoner in, an older guy to act as interpreter, he seemed to spend all his time telling them what to say. 'The bottom line is, Vic, they don't give a fuck. The longer they're in here, the longer their so-called fucking families can claim benefit. Some of these arseholes are making more than we are. The system's fucked and they know it.'

Maybe the whole of the Police and Prison and Immigration

Services read the Daily Mail. *On the other hand, these guys were in the front line so if anybody knew who was winning, they did –*

'What they say, these reports?'

'They said you slipped on the wet floor, Doochy. As you went down you accidentally fell against the door and it slammed and locked shut. They all said it looked as if you'd knocked yourself out and seemed to be having some kind of fit. All they were trying to do was bring you round.'

'Heh heh heh.' Doochy leaned back and closed his eyes. 'You know what the dumb fuckers do? They shit in the drains an' use the heads for drinkin' fountains. Oh Victa, ain't it all a fuck?'

'They didn't smack you up for fuck-all, Doochy.'

'Victa, ever'body blows the whistle on somebody. In New York it was the Jamaicans. They dump me, Victa. You deliver and they dump you. Over here same with the posses. Ever'body nice till the split. Then you on you own. You bring it in, you watch over it – they get their hands on it, they dump you. Same all over, Afghani, fuckin' Turk – fuckin' Turk the wors' of all, no shit. Game over, they blow the whistle an' you can fuck off black boy . . . Yeah . . . Diff'rence is this time I got the whistle, Victa. This time Doochy callin' the shots, hear what I'm sayin'?'

'Dangerous game, kid, you against them. You need any help –'

'Who from? You? A cop? Heh heh heh.'

Once again Doochy slept until lunchtime.

Lasagne, chips, peas, rice pudding. He ate the chips and peas and handed the tray back to Vic.

All through the afternoon, Vic watched high white cumulus speed past and down the wire-mesh glass. Later, heavy grey clouds piled in from the west and flattened down into a dark squall-hung mass. Within seconds, eddies of hard rain were smacking against the glass like handfuls of gravel.

Doochy's eyes opened briefly. 'What a fuckin' countree, man.' He closed them again and his breathing, apart from the hacking and throat-clearing, became regular. Vic stood up to stretch his legs: five paces across the sickbay, five paces back. He could feel the lift and fall of the ship under his feet and the hull graunch up against the chains in the swell.

At half five, with the sky outside dark as night, a full south-westerly gale moaning and howling through every vent and sending waves slam-bang up over the superstructure, Vic's mobile beeped.

'Vic?'

'Hello Sam.'

'Any joy?'

'Not a lot.'

'He still asleep?'

'Yeah.'

'Good. When's he wake up?'

'When he's had his evening joint.'

'Jesus Christ Vic –'

'What?'

'What's that fucking noise?'

'Bit blowy at the moment.'

'Sounds like mother-in-law having a fucking orgasm.'

'Only the wind.'

'That's what she told the vicar.'

Either Sam had been drinking or he was in a good mood.

'What's happened, Sam?'

He heard Sam take a deep self-satisfied breath and guessed he was smoking one of the confiscated Cohibas the Customs guys occasionally pushed his way. 'Tell you the truth, Vic, I've been in this three-way video conference.'

'Fucking hell, Sam. I never knew we had kit like that.'

'We haven't. Had to book a suite in the Ramada.'

'Trebles all round then.'

'Yeah. Satellite takes a fucking age to set up, mind.'

'So you got a good lunch out of it?'

'Middling. Claret was the usual crap.'

'Who else was in on this three-way deal?'

'Me, the London Guys from the Met, Augustin Raveneau.'

'Who?'

'Superintendent Northern Division, Royal St Lucia Police.'

' "Royal"?'

'Oh yeah. You should see their fucking kit, Vic. Sand jackets, staff tabs, epaulettes, fucking great Smith & Wessons – they look like five-star fucking generals and that's only the sergeants. And the size of these blokes. Augustin's as big as Cassius Clay –'

'Mohammad Ali, Sam –'

'And his sidekicks look like Mike Tyson.'

Like a lot of verbal bullies, Sam was attracted by the appearance of brute physical force. Add in guns and uniforms and Sam was well on the way to becoming a happy-clappy fascist.

He went on to tell Vic that his new mate Augustin had not only been to Bramshill Police College but he'd been asked back to lecture there. Sam, as Vic knew, had done neither, and Sam was impressed. In fact, in Vic's opinion, he was over-impressed; Vic found himself wondering why. The answer came after Sam had outlined how the St Lucians were tackling the problem of becoming the cocaine junction of the Caribbean. According to Sam, they had a small force of specially trained men, a fleet of fifty-knot rigid inflatable boats they called RIBs, plus hardware ranging from M16s and Uzi automatics to bow-mounted explosive harpoons. All in all, said Sam, it scared seven shades of shit out of the cocaine fucking cowboys. Then he said, 'Guess what, Vic. Augustin's asked me over on a three-week factfinder, see how they do things. All expenses paid.'

'You going?'

'Thinking about it.'

'You know what Thought did, don't you, Sam?'

'You know what your trouble is, don't you, Hallam?'

'What's that, Sam?'

'You think you're a right fucking smartarse and you're not.'

'So how did the other thing go?'

'What other thing?'

'All the safe-house stuff.'

'Oh yeah. No problem. There's a Seamen's Mission top of Castries overlooking the harbour. Your mate can watch the cruise ships going in and out. Five thousand Yanks a day, apparently.'

'It's all set up, then?'

'More or less.'

Alarm bells ringing. 'What does "more or less" mean, exactly?'

'Well, we're having a bit of an argy-bargy with the Home Office over who pays for the repatriation flight, but you don't have to tell your mate that, it's all agreed in principle –'

'Anything else I don't have to tell him?'

'Vic, your job is to get the griff on the drop, that's all.'

'Sam – is there anything else I don't have to tell him?'

'Augustin says your mate won't know about the Mission. Part of it's now a hospice for leprosy, but it's all right, Vic, you can't catch it, apparently, so personally I wouldn't tell him.'

'Sam –'

'That's all, Vic. Christ sake do as you're told for once.'

'Cheers, Sam.' Vic switched off his mobile, looked over at Doochy. He was still asleep, breathing like an asthmatic.

In the passageway outside the food trolley was starting to make its run.

'It's all right, Vic, you can't catch it, apparently —'

9

'Suppertime, Doochy.'

'Yeah.' Doochy pushed himself up. 'What we got?'

Vic looked. 'Beef curry, rice, apricots. And they've given you a banana.'

'Halle-fuckin'-lujah. It say where it from?'

'I haven't asked it.'

'Hey, Victa, you gettin' the drift, man. Sometimes they got stickers on.'

Vic turned the banana over. 'Oh yeah, Costa Rica.'

'All Yank crap man. They big but they ain't got no taste.'

'Just like the Yanks then.'

'Heh heh heh. You talkin' the talk, Victa.' Doochy paused before digging his fork into the curry. 'Thing is, can you walk the walk?'

'That supposed to mean?'

'I hear you onna mobile. Talkin' to some big-up or other. You know what, Victa? You ain't got no respec' – no respec' for you superiars. No respec' at all. Heh heh heh.'

'I was talking about you, Doochy.'

'I figured.'

'You better eat first.'

'That bad, is it?'

'I wouldn't say that, no.'

'So?'

Vic watched Doochy ploughing into the curry. It looked as if he was starting to get his appetite back. It was three days since he had got hammered. Three days and nights on painkillers: with a hard case like Doochy, HIV or not, it was possible he was into recovery. And if he wasn't, tough shit, it was worth the risk.

'I'm not going to bullshit you, Doochy. What we're talking about is a deal.'

Doochy chewed and nodded, laid down his fork, picked up the banana and split it lengthways with his thumb. 'Everythin's a deal, man.'

'You said you wanted to go home and I believed you. You said what you wanted most of all was to get back to St Lucia. You remember that, Doochy?'

Doochy watched the rain streaming down the wire-mesh glass and nodded. 'I ain' changed my mind, Victa.'

'Well, there could be a way.'

'No shit?'

'You finished with the tray?'

'Yeah.'

As Vic reached for the plastic tray, Doochy laid his dry cold fingers on the back of Vic's hand: 'I take the apricots later.'

'I'll put 'em in your mug, okay?'

'Thanks, man.' As Vic spooned the apricots and juice out of the indentation in the tray into a ridged translucent plastic mug, Doochy said, 'Why you doin' this, Victa?'

'My job.'

Doochy hissed through his teeth and lay back on his pillows with his thin arms clasped behind his head. 'You white guys . . .'

'This is the deal, kid. You can say yes or no, but this is what I'm authorised to offer you. We can put you on a Protected Witness Programme and have you flown home to a secure destination. Thing is, you think you'll be safe in St Lucia?'

Doochy grinned. 'Safe as anywhere, man. Least I ain' gonna sound like a Bajan –'

'I'm not talking about that, Doochy. If you got some kind of deal set up with whoever and you blow the whistle on 'em, sooner or later they're going to know, and my guess is sooner rather than later.'

Doochy grinned. 'Yeah. What I figured. They dump on me, I dump on them, show them how it is. Let them eat shit like I had to. Thass life, Victa –'

'Yeah, but even if we get them all banged up, they got associates, Doochy.'

Still grinning. 'Yeah.'

'Associates with guns, Doochy. I'm talking Men Will Call.'

'Victa, you think you know this deal an' you don't. You know fuck. You ain' bin stuck in this stinkin' joint day afta day, week afta week nothin' to do but figure. I'm talkin' before I got beat up now –'

'So?'

The grin widening right across his face. 'An' while I'm layin' in this shithole I got me an idea. I got me a Big Idea, Victa. A real biggie – one ain' never been done before –'

'And you've got it all set up?'

'One call an' we ready to roll.'

'You know what I think, kid?'

'Don' matter shit what you think –'

'I think you're fucked, Doochy.' Vic watched him trying to keep the grin going. 'And I think you know you're fucked, don't you? These guys kick shit out of you, they know something. You got a leak somewhere. This game, you got leaks, kid, you're sunk. You know that don't you? Or you already got your money up front?'

'Shit, man – you think I'd be talkin' to you?'

'The minute you walk out of here and make that call, you're dead, Doochy.'

'Yeah. Maybe.'

'Even if we get you out and away, it won't stop 'em looking for you.'

Doochy sucked air through his teeth. 'I got people I know. Guys back home jus' waitin' fer to lash up a white man, stick 'im an' skank 'im an' feed 'im to the wild hog up inna hills. Them pigs chomp 'im up good, shoes an' all –'

'How about Yardies?'

Doochy grinned. 'Them too – they ain' got the patois –'

Time to start pulling in the net. 'Anyway, it's your life, Doochy. You'll have new papers, new identity –'

'I'm still gonna be the same old Doochy, man.'

'Up to you, kid, but you got a record long as your arm. You want that following you round?'

'Hey, Victa, can you do that?'

'It's part of the protection procedure.' They were both grinning now: 'You get to turn over a new leaf.'

'Cool . . .'

'And you get enough money to get by on.'

'Man I jus' died and gone to heaven . . . For how long?'

'Not up to me.'

'Wish to fuck it was, Victa. You know that?'

'You and me both.' Vic judged it was time to bring Doochy back down and lay on him what this deal was all about. 'The bottom line on this one is, you and I don't fucking count. Never mind the Big fucking Idea, all that matters is you got certain information, a place and a time, the people you're dealing with don't want you to sell. My people want me to buy that information. Apart from that, these guys, and I mean your guys *and* mine, Doochy, wouldn't piss on us if we were on fire.'

'Heh heh heh. Ain't that the truth?'

'Far as my lot are concerned, they'd probably stand round the flames warming their fucking hands, knocking back the free Scotch and saying, "Thank fuck that's got rid of that awkward old bastard." '

'You ain't so old, Victa.'

'Terms of usefulness we're both past our sell-by date.'

'Can I ast you somethin'?' Doochy leaned forward. 'Why a fuck you ever wanta be a cop when you coulda been *yo bõ volé*?'

'A what?'

'You got a lot a natural cunnin' in you, Victa. You can spin a lie smooth as silk. You coulda been *yo bõ volé* – thass the patois, Victa – St Lucian for one hell of a tief.'

'Oh, right –'

'So why didn' you?'

'Tell you the truth, I think it would've broke my old man's heart.'

'There you go again, man –'

'You still think I'm conning you, don't you, Doochy?'

'Man, I wish I fuckin' knew. Heh heh heh.'

'Okay, let me spell it out. You're ill, you want to go back home. Whether you're going to die or not, or get killed or not, you don't know, I don't know. But regardless of what I do for a living, I happen to think it's a good idea. It's of benefit to you, and it's of benefit to me. So I put it to my boss, and he, because he's come up with fuck-all else –'

'Heh heh heh –'

'– he puts it to his bosses, and they set up a conference, by satellite video link –'

'What a fuck –'

'Don't ask, Doochy, I wasn't there. But they get on to one of the top cops in St Lucia, a guy called Augustin Raveneau –'

'Yeah, I know the Raveneau fam'ly. Come from Dennery, town on a west coast –'

'And he says, yeah, there's this Seamen's Mission he can get to take you –'

'Yeah, I know the Mission. Nice place, looks out over the harbour, you get a nice fresh clean sea breeze up there –'

'So they said. But what you don't know, Doochy, and what they don't want me to tell you, is that part of this Mission is now a hospice for victims of leprosy.'

'Holy fuck, man –'

Vic sat on Doochy's bunk. 'The point is, Doochy, would I have told you that if I was lying through my fucking teeth? If all I wanted was some dope about a coke or heroin drop?'

Doochy shook his head, looked defeated. After a while, he said, 'Was gonna be smack for crack, man.'

'Smack for crack?'

'Yeah. No money, no comebacks.'

'Barter?'

'Yeah. Nothin' to wash, nothin' to trace, both sides uppin' their profit 'cos they ain' no middle guy.'

'What about you?'

'They knock me down, Victa. I ast five, they offer 'alf a one per cent. An' that include me fixin' the set-up on the drop an' all that stuff. Whole idea in this game is you get in an' out fast, Victa, no messin' . . . Mean fuckers haskin' to get dumped –'

'But you took it?' Doochy nodded. 'That the Big Idea?'

'Was. You right, Victa – I knowed I was fucked minute I see them comin' through the door with them big lumps a cable.'

'Doochy – suppose I said fuck the smack, fuck the crack, all I want to see is the back of this fucking shithole and you on your way to sunny St Lucia?' Leaning in close: 'Or d'you think that's a fucking lie as well?'

Doochy said, 'I don' know man, you too fuckin' smart for me. You wore me down, man, you too fuckin' *nice* –'

Vic stood up. 'I'm going for my supper now. You have a smoke and think about it.'

'Yeah. I'll do that.'

'See if you can come up with some other place we can get you into, some convalescent joint where you can get some decent food and people to look after you till you get back on your feet –'

'Yeah. Mus' be some place.' For a moment, Doochy went inside himself; then he looked up, his bony face and hollowed eyes beseeching Vic, his voice unsteady: 'You my main man, Victa –'

A drenching black wave swept over Vic; he'd had

the feeling before: it always came when death was knocking at the door –

The kid's going to die, Hallam, and you're still stringing him along, still making promises you probably can't fucking keep – and the poor cunt still thinks you're too fucking 'nice' . . .

'. . . I'll see if we can scratch up some extra money.'

Doochy looked up at him. 'We talkin' reward money here?'

'That's the deal, kid. Everything you get you fucking earn.'

'Yeah.'

'See you soon.'

'Yeah. Take care, Victa.'

Vic double-locked the sickbay door behind him, leaned back against it, and waited for the black wave to pass over.

At the far end of the passageway, the night staff were starting their rounds, and the drugs trolley, piled high with Doochy's notes and pushed by a hefty ginger-haired male nurse, clanked along the metalled decking.

10

It was chicken provençale: a boiled grey-skinned leg in a mush of chopped tomatoes and mushrooms. Any other night he would have eaten it but tonight he felt a need to get back to Doochy. After five minutes, he stubbed out his Marlboro in a paint-tin-lid ashtray and left.

The sickbay door was on the latch.

Fuck –

There was a kind of soft resistance.

He put his shoulder down and shoved.

The metal door gave way.

Oh fuck –

Doochy was on the floor inside the door and a short skinny dark-haired guy in a white coat was discharging a hypodermic into the hard shrivelled muscle of Doochy's arse.

'You bastard!'

Vic grabbed the skinny guy round the neck and shoulders. As he hauled him off, the man twisted round and tried to stab the needle in Vic's face. Vic caught hold of his wiry black-haired forearm and forced it back. Spray from the needle shot into Vic's eyes and mouth. Blinded, the skin round his eyes and mouth burning, Vic hung on and tried to break the guy's arm across his knee.

He heard the syringe clatter on the metalled floor then the skinny guy writhed down out of Vic's grasp on to the floor. Vic caught him again by falling on him. He felt legs kicking him in the guts and chest. The bastard was trying to drag himself through the doorframe into the passageway. Vic, knowing he was losing him, stretched out a hand and grabbed the chipped edge of the metal door. He slammed it with all his strength. A pulpy crunching noise like an apple being crushed, then a grunt, a smell of blood, and the skinny guy went limp.

Vic felt his way over to Doochy. 'How you doing, kid?'

Doochy was making brief gasping noises as if someone were repeatedly punching him in the stomach. 'Victa?'

'What is it kid, where's it hurt?'

'Anh . . . Ah . . . Aa . . . pipe . . .'

'What?'

'A . . . pipe –'

Vic felt him shudder.

He was lying on his back staring up at a bright white circular light. There was something like a strip of freezing cold gauze lying across his eyes, and a clean smell, like witch hazel, but he could still see the bright white light.

Now it was turning red.

Neon red.

Intensifying until it was hard and bright as a coke fire.

The disc hollowing into a rotating 'O' . . .

Letters appearing to the left: 'DISC' . . .

More letters appearing to the right: 'VERY' . . .

Then merging together on the ceiling . . .

Hanging above his head, a word, in foot-high letters: DISCOVERY . . .

'Vic. Come on, Vic. Come on –' A hand shaking his shoulder; fingers peeling off the strip of gauze; his eyes focusing . . .

Ellie was looking down on him, lips pursed, eyes hot and blue as acetylene, voice peremptory: 'Come on, Vic.'

He was lying in a hospital bed. There were screens round him. They had big red-and-orange chrysanthemums printed on them. His mouth was burning. It was like when he and Joe had tried drinking petrol when he was a kid –

'Vic, can you see me?'

'What?'

'Can you see me?'

'I could if you turned that fucking light out.'

A hand moved across his vision, pushed an angled bed light up and off his face.

'That better?'

'Yeah. What are you doing here?'

'I work here.'

'What?'

'You're in A&E, Dorset County Hospital. This is an examination room so the staff can keep an eye on you from the nurses' station.'

'Oh –'

'I'm not supposed to be on this ward, I'm on Kimmeridge, but they told me.'

'Oh –'

'D'you understand what I'm saying, Vic?'

'Yeah, you're on Kimmeridge but they told you.'

He watched Ellie pick up his chart from the foot of the bed and pull a chrome Paper Mate from her breast pocket. 'What day is it?'

'Tuesday.'

'Time?'

'About seven . . . ?'

'When?'

'In the evening –'

'Who's the Prime Minister?'

Oh fuck –

'Come on, Vic –'

'It's – it's that guy – that guy who smiles a lot but looks nervous – as if he's just been caught out –'

'What's his name?'

'Blair. Yeah – Tony Blair –'

Ellie leaned down and kissed him on the forehead. She smelled, as she always did, of oatmeal and Badedas. 'You bugger.' Smiling to herself she tucked the crisp sheet neatly round his bare chest.

'Why? What have I done now?'

'It's half seven on Wednesday morning, Vic.'

'You what?'

'Don't forget. The doctors do their rounds at eight. I've got to go now. Bye love.'

'Bye.' As soon as he closed his eyes his head began to swim. It wasn't like a hangover when the walls began to spin first one way then the other: this was quite a pleasant sensation, like going slowly down a spiral water-chute into a warm bath. He felt confident, half drunk, unusually passive and at peace. Even the burning feeling was fading into a cold dental numbness.

He was vaguely sad he couldn't see the letters of fire any more: he had enjoyed that – it was like watching fireworks as a kid and seeing the final GOODBYE FOLKS! blazing into life – but it didn't really matter. Nothing mattered . . . What did that young cop who quit to become a Buddhist monk used to say? 'Nothing matters very much and very little matters at all.'

Yeah, that was about it –

Then the door clicked open and three dark-haired men in white coats came in and Vic found he was sitting up in bed with his fists raised in front of him: 'What the fuck –?'

A nurse in a pale blue dress like Ellie's came forward from behind the three men and took hold of his fists. Her hands were warm and she was smiling: 'It's all right Sergeant Hallam, there's nothing to worry about.'

'What?'

The staff nurse pulled out the backrest, plumped

up his pillows and eased his head gently back. 'How's that?'

'What . . . Oh, fine –'

'All Mr Karkouri wants to do is have a look at you.' She turned away and Vic heard her murmur something about him being 'hypertensive'. One of the two younger doctors picked up Vic's notes, clicked his Bic and made a brief entry.

Mr Karkouri's hospital ID said he was a consultant neurologist. A small, precise, soft spoken man in his forties, he tested Vic's physical reactions from his toes to the pupils of his eyes and quizzed him thoroughly about the exact sequence of events. Simultaneously, his younger colleagues hooked Vic up to a wheeled electronic monitor which measured his pulse, blood pressure and temperature from an attachment to his middle finger. Vic found himself describing an incident which seemed to have happened to someone else. Not only that, his recollection was episodic, and when he apologised that all he seemed to be able to recall was a set of edited highlights, Mr Karkouri smiled and said that this sort of suppression was not unusual: it could be the result of either trauma or residual narcosis and almost certainly Vic's recall would improve with the passage of time. When Vic asked him about the letters of fire spelling out the word DISCOVERY he said that hallucinations were not uncommon under anaesthesia and that many adults and even children reported seeing cartoon characters such as Mickey Mouse, Tom and Jerry or the

Simpsons. As for the word itself, Mr Karkouri said that some types of psychologist might say it represented an 'as yet unrecovered memory'. Mr Karkouri smiled at his junior colleagues as he said this and Vic got the impression neither he nor they thought very much of psychology. All the same he went on to ask Vic about the day, the time and the name of the Prime Minister.

After conferring with the staff nurse about further scans and tests, Mr Karkouri turned back to Vic. 'Now, Sergeant Hallam, do you have any questions you would like to ask?'

'The obvious one is when do I get out?'

'Depending on tests possibly tonight, probably tomorrow.'

'So what happened to me then? Why did I pass out?'

'As far as we can tell you seem to have ingested or absorbed a combination of pethidine and rohypnol. Either would put you out – pethidine is a powerful opiate and analgesic and rohypnol, as you may know, is commonly known as the date-rape drug.'

'What about Doochy – Mr Duchene?'

'Mr Duchene was injected. He received a far greater dose than you and unfortunately, given his weakened condition, it proved fatal.'

'I see. And the other guy, the one that did it?'

'Sustained severe skull fracture and massive cerebral haemorrhage.'

'Is he dead?'

'I'm afraid so.'

'Thank you, doctor.'

11

After an EEG, an ECG, a tomographic scan that took pictures of his brain in slices, and four separate blood tests, it was lunchtime: shepherd's pie and plum-and-apple crumble. The food was ten times better than the stodge you got on the *Aware*; Vic, lying on his bed replete and fully dressed except for his shoes, idly debated whether diet should be part of prisoners' punishment. On the one hand the huge carbohydrate overload was calculated to keep the buggers quiet; on the other, they had more rows, riots and lock-ins over food than anything else . . .

He was drifting off into an indeterminate doze when the door clicked open and a voice said, 'Seventy-two miles in the pissing rain and the cunt's lying there like Sleeping fucking Beauty.'

Vic opened his eyes. 'Hallo Sam.'

'You all right? *Compos mentis*?'

'Fine.'

'Good.' Sam pulled a voice-operated Minidisc recorder out of his pocket, and set it on Vic's bedside table. 'This interview fourteen-ten May five, Dorset County Hospital, self Superintendent Richardson, subject DS Hallam.' Sam stopped the recording, wound back, played it over and, with his finger poised over RECORD, said, 'I suppose you know there'll be an inquiry?'

'Tell you the truth, I hadn't thought about it –'

'Well think about it now. Because thanks to you we've lost our two best witnesses.' Sam pressed RECORD. 'Now then in your own words, Sergeant Hallam –'

'Starting from when?'

'Let's say from events leading up to the assault of the evening of May four and continuing through to the consequences at the present time as far as you are aware.'

Vic leaned back on his pillows, shuffling the sequence of events into basic chronological order, but all the time thinking what a bastard Sam was. First sign of trouble and the only thing on his mind was how to save his own arse.

'Fuck,' said Sam.

'What?'

'Fucking thing's stopped.'

'No it hasn't. It's voice-operated.'

'Oh yeah. Go on then.'

Vic went through it from his first meeting with Doochy to leaving his chicken provençale to hearing from Mr Karkouri that the dark skinny guy was dead.

Sam switched to PAUSE. 'And that's it, is it?'

'Enough, isn't it?'

'Enough to get you suspended, yeah.' It took Sam several attempts to switch the voice recorder off.

'That would have happened anyway. With an inquiry, it's automatic –'

'You don't get it do you, Vic? I don't want you suspended even if you *are* fucking suspended –'

'Meaning what?'

'You go on working – you're a sleeper, for Christ sake, who's going to fucking know?'

'Me and you for a start. Plus the guys on the inquiry. They find out and we're both in the shit.'

'Put your shoes on, Vic, I need some fresh air.'

They moved through the pale-brick and painted-steel hospital walkways until they came to a mobile of twenty-foot pencil-shapes surrounded by a carved stone wall. The mobile swung slowly, gleaming in the drizzle. They stood under an entrance awning. Underneath the NO SMOKING sign was a black metal bin filled with sand and half-buried cigarette ends.

Sam said, 'Before I came to see you I went to see the lads in mortuary.'

'Where?'

'Here, you pillock. They don't like keeping bodies in the Verne. Upsets the inmates. Anyway this guy Willoughby was there, the police pathologist. Tall, striped suit, swept-back silver hair, looks like some fucking professor off the telly. Know him?'

'No.'

'One of these supercilious bastards enjoys gutting stiffs, likes to see if he can get you to throw up. Prat.' Sam took out a Henri Wintermans packet; across the top corner in yellow, SAMPLE PACK. Vic guessed it was another freebie and watched Sam light up. The smoke from the half-corona hung and layered in the damp air. 'Anyway he shows me your mate and this skinny guy. Skinny guy's skull was caved in both sides, Vic. You could see his brains poking out the top of his head like fucking cauliflower cheese.'

'Really.'

'You don't seem, what shall I say, overly concerned, Vic.'

'I'm not. They got a name for him yet?'

'Yeah. Some fucking Balkanian or other.'

'Not one of the ones in solitary?'

'No, some other fucker.'

'On board or from outside?'

'Oh, he was on board all right.'

'What for?'

'Drugs over here, armed robbery and torturing his fellow countrymen over there. Was in one of their Security Forces, claimed he was in danger of his life.'

'We know how he got into sickbay?'

'I'll get to that later.' Sam blew out another grey cloud and looked at the lit end to see if it was burning evenly. 'The important thing for you now, Vic – this Willoughby prat says we're looking at undue force.'

'Does he?'

'Yeah.' Sam took out his pocket book. ' "Undue and excessive force on the part of the officer involved".'

'It was him or me, Sam.'

'Never goes down well, Vic. Specially with this Balkanian fuckpig already being in custody.'

Vic knew Sam was putting the arm on him: do as I say, Vic, or you'll be on your own facing charges of manslaughter, possible murder, dismissal and no fucking pension. Plus, if it all turned to shit Sam would play the 'I-know-nothing-I'm-from Barcelona' defence and walk away leaving Vic to carry the can.

Which by this time, Hallam, would be full to overflowing –

'What d'you think we should do, Sam?'

Sam, smiling his lipless winner's smile: 'All we need to do, Vic, is go on as we are. Ignore this fucking suspension and get Calder down to deal with Mr fartarse fucking Willoughby.'

Calder was the Bristol police pathologist.

As usual Sam had it all worked out.

Vic forced a grin. 'Fair enough.'

'You'll do it?'

'Not much option, have I?'

'Not a lot.'

'What else do we know, Sam?'

'Well, I had a word with your Mr Khazi –'

'Karkouri –'

'And he gave me a print-out of the analysis of the stuff left in the syringe –'

'Was there any?'

'Always a drop, Vic. I faxed it off to the labs at the Met.'

'Any joy?'

'This Met techie bloke comes back on the phone and he's laughing his bollocks off –'

'Laughing?'

'I say what's so fucking funny and he says it's what they call the Bulgarian truth drug, and I say why Bulgarian, and he says because it never fucking works –'

'So Doochy died for fuck-all then?'

'You could say that.'

I don' wanna die in this cold damn frien'less countree –

'Poor bastard.'

'If you say so, Vic.'

'So how did this guy get to him? When I left I locked the fucking door –'

'You sure of that?'

Vic saw himself double-locking the sickbay door, leaning against it and waiting for the black wave to pass . . .

'Positive.'

'Hundred per cent?'

'Christ sake Sam, you know what these places are like – you lock, you double-lock, you check, you double-check –'

'So who else has keys?'

'The night staff.'

'Who are?'

'Well, because there's only Doochy –'

Was only Doochy.

'Go on Vic.'

'Because there was only Doochy in sickbay they had two officers doing the rounds, one duty nurse on station opposite sickbay. They'd started the drug run when I went off for supper.'

'Which is when?'

'Half six to seven – except I came back early –'

'They all have keys?'

'Yes. The nurse runs an hourly check through the inspection hatch – any emergency he rings the alarm outside sickbay for officer-assist before entering –'

'There were no keys on the body, Vic.'

'What?'

'The guy you jumped. Had no keys. So that leaves the nurse and the two officers. That's three leads for a start. You come up with anything?'

'I'd practically got Doochy signed up.'

'Fuck.'

'Why I went back early.'

'Bastard.' Sam chewed the end of the half-corona, spat out bits of soggy black leaf. 'So what was the deal?'

'For him or for us?'

'Us. Too late for him. Come on, Vic. Get a fucking grip –'

'Barter.'

'Barter?'

' "Smack for crack" he called it. Said it was his Big Idea.'

'I don't get it.'

'You meet, you swap an agreed amount of smack for an agreed amount of crack. No money means no comebacks. No need to raise it, launder it, risk it being traced or knocked off. You up your profits and you double your market. You're in both games, and not only that – once you've eliminated the middle guys you're getting Grade A stuff because nobody's cutting it before you do.'

'What was your mate getting out of it?'

'Half a per cent.'

'Chickenshit.'

'Yeah, they screwed him down from five.'

'As they do.'

'Still fifty grand on a ten-mil deal.'

'Yeah.' Sam stuffed the half-corona in the wet sand bin. 'If these fuckers ever start to trust each other we're in deep shit.'

'Way I see it, somebody's already leaked it.'

'How come?'

'The guys who beat him up wanted in. They saw they were being left out of the loop and if this kind of deal took off they'd be dead in the water. They knew Doochy'd got the contacts to set something up, otherwise why bother with him? Up to then he'd only been the minder, the fall guy who delivered the stuff, got paid peanuts and told to fuck off up the road.'

'Can't tell with these fucking Balkanians. They're all fucking psychos.'

'Doesn't mean to say they're fucking stupid –'

'So now you're saying there's a third party involved?'

'Yes –'

'A third party and we don't even know who the other two are. We don't know who's running the crack and we don't know who's running the smack.

That's why I sent you down here, Vic, and so far it seems to me you've found out fuck-all –'

'Look Sam, I was with the kid for two fucking days. Doochy *knew* he'd fucked up. He didn't want to believe it because it was his last fucking chance to make his stash but he knew all right. Somebody blew it to those guys and they tried to beat it out of him. He might've kept schtum but he knew he was fucked. Otherwise I'd never have had him on the edge. Then they tried to drug it out of him and OD'd the poor fucker.'

'And that's what you think happened?'

'I *know*, Sam. I was fucking *there* –'

Sam sniffed and wiped the end of his nose between thumb and forefinger. 'You offer him money?'

'I said he'd have enough to get by on.'

'You shouldn't have done that, Vic. You'd got no authority.'

'Fuck's sake Sam, two blokes dead and all you can think of is saving your fucking arse –'

'I'll pretend you didn't say that, Sergeant.'

'All I did was tell the poor cunt there'd be reward money. He'd have earned every fucking penny –'

'Nobody's talking reward money any more, Vic. Home Office and the Met don't want the great British public thinking we're lobbing out thousands of pounds to hardened fucking criminals.'

'Fucking hell, Sam –'

'Christ sake Vic, look at it from my point of view for once. This fucking pathologist's saying undue and excessive force, you've got no drop, no place, no time, nobody to back up this fucking barter story and you're saying you practically had the kid turned. Looks like you're the one saving your arse Hallam.'

'Bollocks.'

Sam grinned, slapped his hand on Vic's shoulder. 'Come on, mate, let's go and have a look at the stiffs.'

Don't call me fucking mate –

They walked past the twenty-foot pencil shapes. They were still dripping, still swinging aimless ellipses against the sky. Sam looked up: 'What a daft waste of public money.'

'It's called art, Sam.'

'Yeah. With a capital F.' From twenty yards off Sam pressed the Saab's key-fob. The car's sidelights flickered three times and Sam smiled with satisfaction. 'Anything else?'

'What?'

'This Balkanian fuckpig stabbed the hypo in the kid's arse, then what?'

Vic thought back to Doochy lying face down, dying on the sickbay floor. 'He was trying to say something.'

'Now he tells me. What?'

' "A pipe." What it sounded like anyway. Last thing he said. Only thing he said –'

' "A pipe"?'

'Yeah. Said it three, four times. Struggling to get it out.'

'Did he have a pipe? A crack pipe, anything like that?'

'No. He rolled joints, smoked Camel Lights.'

'Means fuck-all to me then. You?'

'Not so far, no.'

All the same I owe you one, Doochy.

By the time they drove out of the hospital car park and waited in traffic on the access road, the drizzle had stopped and a watery sun had thrown a burning rainbow across the grey cloud over Maiden Castle.

'There you are Vic,' said Sam 'Your lucky day.'

12

In the Saab, Sam said, 'These three, the prison officers and this male nurse. They know you're a copper?'

'Prison officers definitely. The nurse probably.'

'Why probably?'

'One, he's on duty with them. Two, there's only Doochy in sickbay. The nurse is on station opposite. Doochy's got one-to-one nursing so what do they want a ward orderly for? Bound to put his nose out.'

'You talk to him at all?'

'Only to say goodnight when I signed off. You got to remember, Sam, the evening was the only time Doochy was awake so that was the only time I could talk to him.'

'What's he like, this nurse?'

'Big ginger-haired kiddie. Heavy on his feet. Doesn't say much, listens to his MP3 all the time. Different to the day bloke.'

'In what way?'

'Scouser in his forties. Allie. Little dark bloke, built like a jockey. One of these blokes can't stop talking, can't stand still. Always wanting to do things for you – the cons love him –'

'He bent?'

'Don't think so, just one of these over-anxious little guys, likes to be liked. Always rabbiting on about his mother –'

'He live with her?'

'Must do.'

'There y'are then. Bent.'

There was no point in arguing. 'Anyway, when I was on he used to make tea and toast in the sluice, bring it over eleven o'clock and four o'clock. Used to bring Doochy the *Sun* and *Daily Sport*, loved nattering to him –'

'Liked a bit of black did he?'

Fuck off, Sam –

'What about the night bloke?'

'Chalk and cheese. Never said a word. Allie reckoned all night nurses were fucking morose by nature. But I was only on duty with him from seven to ten at night.'

'He have a name?'

'Steven Chant on his ID.'

'Who opened up?'

'He did. As the nurse in charge.'

When they reached the mortuary car park Sam took the key out of the ignition and sat in the Saab spinning the key-fob round his finger. When they got out he leaned on the roof and said, 'You can't do it, Vic.'

The mortuary block was on the north side of the hospital, close to the twenty-four-hour traffic on the

A35 trunk route to Cornwall. It was windowless and unsignposted on the outside but a giveaway matt-black air-conditioning system squatted on its flat roof. As they walked down a flight of steps to the semi-underground entrance, Sam said the traffic noise would be the last of the poor buggers' worries.

Vic said, 'So what d'you mean, I can't do it?'

Sam checked out the air-locked entrance before replying. 'Suppose it *was* one of these three left the sickbay door open. You start asking questions now, all their defence has to say is you've compromised the inquiry by acting on your own behalf without authority and that's your evidence fucked in toto.'

'I already told you that,' said Vic.

'Well now I'm telling you, smartarse.'

'So if not me, who? You can't leave it to an internal.'

'I'm thinking about it.' Sam pressed a buzzer and held his ID up to a CCTV camera. 'Apart from anything else, Vic, if you found out who it was you might lay one on him.'

I owe you one, Doochy.

Inside, the same old chill and the same old sickly whiff that no amount of formaldehyde, disinfectant or air-con would ever disguise.

The white-wellingtoned attendant led them past the stainless-steel autopsy benches into a tiled side room. On a blue formica table lay a red-zipped opaque plastic pouch. It was A4-sized, barely half full and contained all Doochy's belongings. The attendant asked them to check the contents against a computer print-out. 'If you would make sure everything is absolutely tickety-boo, gentlemen, then perhaps one of you would care to sign in the space provided.'

There was an empty green and gold leather wallet with a resealable plastic gag containing £8.74 attached by paperclip, a watch described as facsimile Singapore Rolex, a pair of CHARMONY FRAME JAPAN 145mm spectacles with one hinge wound round with surgical tape, and a few till receipts. In a separate white envelope was an unopened pack of Durex Fetherlite.

'Ah well,' said Sam, signing for the red-zipped pouch and its contents, 'hope springs eternal –'

'Thank you, gentlemen –'

'Hang on a minute,' said Vic. 'What about clothes?'

'Apart from the post-op gown the gentleman was wearing on admission, there were no clothes.'

'Portland,' said Sam. 'They're still in fucking Portland.'

After Vic had navigated them out on to the A354, Sam tossed the red-zipped pouch on to Vic's lap. 'Pick the bones out of that. They can't do you for investigating Doochy. Why you were there in the first place.'

At the steep downhill hairpin high above Weymouth, Sam said, 'My old man used to make us

get out of the Morris Minor and walk this bend in case
he went over the top –'

'A lot of stuff did. Lorries mostly –'

'Times have changed, Vic.' Then, abruptly: 'What
the fuck's up with Cromer?'

DC John Cromer, twenty-four, had been Vic's
sidekick in Central.

'I don't know, Sam. Haven't spoken to him since I
got down here.'

'I wish you would, Vic.'

'Why?'

'He's had a commendation, promotion to DS, and
ever since then he's been miserable as buggery. I'd got
him down as a high flyer but ever since you left he's
been no fucking use to anyone, no fucking use at all.
Anybody'd think the silly fucker was in love with
you –'

'Not me, Sam –'

'Who then?'

'Palmer Street. That young woman got shot. Opal
Macalpine.'

'Yeah but Cromer got the blokes that did it –'

'She was his girl, Sam. Couldn't keep his hands off
her.'

'What about his fiancée – hairdresser, out
Fishponds way?'

'They weren't getting on. Opal turns up and that's
that.'

'I don't know where you blokes find the fucking
time –'

'Anyway, Opal was the one. Then she got shot. Louise, the hairdresser, took him back. End of story.'

Sam drove in silence along the dual carriageway. 'You think this hairdresser's giving him a bad time?'

'Nothing worse than being forgiven, Sam. Gives them the right to bite your balls off every time you open your mouth.'

'You should know, Vic – oh shit, where the fuck we go now?'

'Left at the roundabout over the top on to the causeway.'

'Got it.' When they were on the causeway, its surface slick with spray and scattered with gravel, Sam said, 'And you think that's it – she's still giving him stick?'

'Worse than that. I think he's still giving himself stick.'

Sam nodded. 'What cunts we all are.'

At the *Aware* Sam parked on the quayside, inside the four-metre chainlink fence, and told Vic to stay in the car. 'No sense them seeing you and me together.'

While he waited, Vic went through the contents of the red-zipped pouch. No photographs. No credit cards. No scraps of addresses. Not even a union card.

Not much for a life: less than a tenner and a bunch of till and Mastercard receipts. They were up to a month old, mostly from Bushells Wines, Weymouth: Barcardi, Pepsi, Camel Lights . . .

Hang on –

Weymouth?

Doochy hadn't left sickbay since he'd arrived so how the fuck did he ever get to Weymouth?

And where the fuck was his bloody Mastercard?

Sam climbed back in the Saab with a black plastic sack and dumped it on Vic's lap. 'All that fucking red tape for a bagful of manky old rags –'

'What about his medical records?'

'They won't release them without Mr fartarse fucking Willoughby's say-so.' He grabbed for the car phone. 'I'm phoning Calder now. Where's your motor?'

'In the staff car park over the fence.'

'Near enough to walk?'

'Course –'

'I'll see you then, Vic –'

'You want me to take the clothes?'

'I don't want them stinking out my car, do I?'

'Right –'

'Oh Vic.' Sam leaned over as Vic dumped the black plastic sack and red-zipped pouch on the wet tarmac: 'I've decided to send Cromer down to handle the inquiry this end –'

'Cromer?'

'Yeah, he's your mucker isn't he? You can bring him up to speed. Any objections?'

'No – fine by me –'

'Good. Now – he'll need somewhere to stay, not

here, not Weymouth, somewhere fucking anonymous –'

'There's St Bride's Seasider Caravan Park –'

'Perfect. He could do with a holiday – getting away from this fucking hairdresser might cheer the young cunt up –'

13

Vic had the soused mackerel and potato salad ready on big white Habitat plates when Ellie came in. Her cheeks were cold from the fresh sea breeze.

'What's that in the fryer?'

'Sea-kale.'

'Never heard of it.'

'Grows outside the front gate.'

'What, that green stuff the dogs piss on?'

'Improves the flavour –'

She looked into the bubbling golden vegetable oil. The pale sea-kale, chopped into quarter-inch strips, was already turning a crisp dark green. 'I'm not eating that.'

'Oh come on, I've washed it, haven't I?'

'You better have.' She laid a thick white plastic bag on the dresser. It was labelled SHARPS ONLY and sealed with Micropore paper tape. 'What's it taste like anyway?'

'Spinach, only nicer. Try a bit.' Vic lifted and shook the container, picked out a curly twist, broke it in half, ate one piece and dangled the other in front of Ellie. She took it off him and nibbled it suspiciously.

'What d'you think?'

'Not bad. More like crunchy seaweed than spinach.'

'You don't get that in Birmingham.'

'I just hope you haven't wasted all that oil.'

'Course not. Only been in five seconds.'

'Who told you about it?'

'Joe. Cath does it for him. What's in the bag?'

'Your stuff from the hospital. You're not supposed to discharge yourself, you know.'

'Phoned 'em, didn't I?'

'Did you call yourself Thompson?'

'I did on the *Aware*, yeah. You have to use a different ID.' Ellie nodded. 'I thought so.'

'Why, what's up, love?'

'You had a couple of visitors after you left.'

'What sort of visitors?'

'Dark, thin-faced. Looking for Mr Thomp-son.'

'Thomp as in Thump?'

'Yes.'

'And?'

Accusing him: 'It *has* started hasn't it, Vic?'

'What else they say?'

'They told the staff nurse they were friends of yours and could they leave a get-well card.'

'Where is it?'

'In the bag.'

Vic tore the bag open. Lying on top of his blood-stained white jacket and dark trousers was a sealed white envelope. Inside was a passport photo of the skinny dark-haired guy who had tried to stab the syringe in his face. On the back, scrawled in capitals:

I SHALL RITERN

14

Losing Opal had hit Cromer hard. It showed in his face, his eyes, his whole body: he had become leaner, paler, harder, as if her death had both wasted and tempered him. Even the attempt at a bleach-blond surfer hairstyle had gone, replaced by a number-three buzzcut and a widow's peak.

'Morning, Vic.'

'You've lost weight, John.'

'Yeah, I've been working out.'

'What the fuck for?'

'Oh, you know, something to do . . .' Then, to cover himself: 'You get too fat-arsed sitting in Central all day long –'

'Come in – Ellie's already gone to work.'

'Thanks.' He stood in the bright newly-furnished sitting room, looking round. 'This is nice – better than that basement shitheap you used to live in.'

'That's the woman's touch –'

'Yeah . . .'

'I'll get the coffee.'

Cromer was standing in the same place when Vic came back in with a couple of blue-and-white-striped mugs. 'Sit down, John.'

'Thanks.' He sniffed at the steam rising from the mug. 'Mm, real coffee.'

They sat facing each other across the irregular two-inch slab of varnished elm Vic and Ellie used as a coffee table.

'So what's been happening?'

Cromer placed his mug on a glass coaster. 'Didn't Ellie have this table in that flat she had in Cornwallis Crescent?'

'Yeah. Landlord said she could have it as a wedding present.' Vic put his own mug down and looked at Cromer. 'You got a copper's memory, John.'

'Nice piece of wood. Not much elm about now.'

'No, not a lot.' Vic leaned forward, elbows on his knees. 'Must have been rough these last few months.'

'Still is.' Looking at Vic dry-eyed, no trace of self-pity.

'I'm sorry mate.'

'Yeah, well, shit happens.'

'And Louise?'

'I left her weeks ago.'

'That's something.'

The start of a fuck-you grin. 'Life as we know it is not possible in Fishponds. Not above that fucking hairdressing salon anyway.'

'Hope for you yet, old son.' Vic felt their relationship, a mixture of piss-taking and camaraderie, stirring back into life.

'I never knew whether she was going to pretend to feel sorry for me or chew my fucking balls off.'

'They all go for the scrotum, John.'

'Anyway, when she finally got hold of the idea I wasn't going to screw the arse off her any more, she threw me out.'

'I thought you said you left her?'

'Let's say I made it easy for her.'

'You're learning, kid. Where are you now?'

'You'll never believe this.'

'What?'

'I've got this bedsit in St Pauls Road, opposite the BBC. Landlord runs this what looks like this dodgy sort of S&M-type club in the basement. Sunday afternoons you get all sorts of weird blokes turning up. All carrying suitcases.'

'You check him out?'

'Had to. I told him if money was changing hands I'd have to report him. He said oh no, they were all weekend volunteers and it was strictly Members Only.' He took a sip of coffee, replaced the mug carefully on the glass coaster. 'Anyway, how's Ellie?'

'Plimming up nicely.'

'Good.'

Vic said, 'So what's all this working-out crap?'

'The landlord lets out the basement to Clifton Taekwondo in the week. They bring their own judo mats. I did taekwondo all through school and college, only packed it in when I joined the Force. Thought I'd take it up again.'

'That where you kick and punch the shit out of each other?'

'Yeah.' Grinning. 'I thought it'd be more fun than S&M.'

'You learn the – what do they call 'em? Pressure points?'

'Yeah.'

'You know they can kill people?'

'You have to learn the *hyung*, the right string of moves first. Plus all sorts of other stuff.'

'Why?'

'You're supposed to develop inner peace and total calm. Mind and body become one. You don't think. You are, you act –'

'And you kill some poor cunt?'

'Old Koreans called it Bringing the Gift.'

'Fucking hell, John.'

Cromer smiled.

After coffee, Vic put the mugs in the sink, took Cromer over to the Seasider Caravan Park, showed him the thirty-six-foot mobile home, said he'd give him time to get sorted then they'd have a chat about the job.

'Fair enough.'

Vic went back to Flask Cottage, washed and dried the mugs, then rang Sam.

'I'm not sure John's up for this, Sam.'

'Course he is. Not still being mardy-arsed, is he?'

'No, it's not that –'

'What then?'

'I just don't think he's had enough time off yet.'

'Vic, he's had the counselling, he's been passed A1 for normal fucking duties –'

'Let me put it like this – d'you think he's stable enough?'

'Who the fuck is? We're all under pressure –'

'He's just not the same bloke –'

'You're a fine one to fucking talk – look how you were when you were getting divorced –'

'What you talking about?'

'I'll tell you what I'm fucking talking about. You were either hung-over, drunk, or walking round like a bear with a sore arse – *and* you slept with the chief witness in a rape case. How fucking stable is that?'

'Even so –'

'Look Vic. All Cromer needs is some normal, ordinary routine police work – and that's all this inquiry is. He talks to the screws, the cons, this ginger-haired kiddie, forensics, everybody – even the fucking prison visitors, because they'll have their fingers all over this one making sure these fucking Balkanians haven't had their prisoners' rights abused. We can't afford to drop any more bricks so you keep your nose out, stick to your mate Doochy and leave the inquiry to Cromer. It's not exactly fucking rocket-science, is it?'

'Shouldn't be –'

'Cromer's basically a good copper – all he needs now is something to get his teeth into –'

'If you say so, Sam.'

'Work. Cures everything. Cheers, Vic.'

'Cheers.'

15

'This is ace, Vic.' Cromer had his feet up on the sun-faded horseshoe banquette watching morning television in the lounge of the mobile home. 'I got a shower, a loo, a kitchen-diner, a bloody great double bed and I can check out all the talent going into the bar without so much as shifting me arse.'

To Vic the brown-and-orange carpeted lounge smelled of dog, old takeaways and hot plastic. 'Glad you like it.'

Cromer opened up his laptop. 'Right, fire away.'

At the end of the briefing, Vic dropped the passport photo of the dark skinny guy on to the keyboard of the laptop. 'According to the mortuary he's called Ramiz.'

Cromer grinned. 'This the guy whose head you mashed?'

'Yeah. Have a look on the back.'

Cromer flipped the photo over with the end of a ballpoint.

'There won't be any prints –'

'Never know –'

'Nurses have handled it – so has Ellie, so have I.'

Cromer leaned forward to look at the words

written on the back. ' "I SHAL RITERN." ' Grinning at Vic. 'He'll be lucky.'

'They're vicious bastards, John.'

'Good. How do we split it?'

'It's all yours. You're the investigating officer. All I'm doing is following up odds and ends on Doochy –'

'The black kid?'

'Yeah.' Vic pulled out the evidence bag containing Doochy's belongings. 'Couple of receipts from a wine shop in Weymouth.'

'What did Sam Richardson say?'

'Keep my nose out, leave it to you. You're the DS on this one, I'm just the dogsbody.'

Without a trace of a smile Cromer said, 'Makes a change, doesn't it?' Cromer tapped away on his laptop, frowning away, tapping some more, then looking up as if surprised Vic was still there. 'Thanks, Vic.'

There was something adrift somewhere: even if Cromer was just feeling his oats, staking out his territory, there was no need to behave like a prat about it. No point in telling Sam either: he'd say it was all just bloody daft tittle-tattle.

Fucking police work –

'Hey Vic!' Joe was stacking pots on the afterdeck of the *Rob Roy*. 'Fancy a couple of hours?'

Vic balanced the idea: putting out to sea, feeling the fresh air and the lift of the swell liberating him . . . Then realising he'd be nagging himself to death all the way out and back.

Fucking Cromer – what was the matter with him?

'Sorry Joe, can't do it.'

'Should've packed it in when I did.'

'Yeah. How d'you get on with Giffen over the outboard?'

'Old Scrump? Peeled three-fifty off a roll as big as your fist nice as pie. Even offered his apologies.'

'Good for you –'

'He wants to hire the boat for a couple of weeks.'

'Money any good?'

'Wouldn't come amiss, Vic, fucking financial state I'm in. I told Scrump I'd have to ask you.'

'Take it, Joe.'

'Why, what's happening?'

'I'm being fucked about, mate. Let's leave it at that.'

Twenty minutes later, Vic had left Ellie a note, changed into his baggy black suit and was on his way to Bristol in the Cavalier.

He reached the Fishponds salon at 12.50. Louise was tinting a customer. The old lady had a yellowish plastic cap on and Louise had teased clumps of white hair through the perforations. The old lady's skin was the colour of parchment and when she closed her eyelids she looked dead. Vic felt embarrassed to be there. Louise picked up on it: 'I've just got this lady to finish then it's my lunch break. You go up, door's on the latch.'

The stairs led out of the back of the salon and as Vic went up he heard the old lady say something about being twenty years younger and both of them cackled.

Vic let himself in. The short hall was floored with blue vinyl tiles pocked with heel marks and led to a blue-grey living room facing Fishponds Road. The two windows had swagged lace curtains with red ties. There was a nubbly oatmeal settee and matching armchair facing a silver widescreen TV by the side of a regency-style Coalectric fire with a rag-rug in front of it.

Louise came in and threw her blue nylon overall on the settee. She was a tall slim young woman with dark hair, a pallid complexion and shadows under her eyes; not unattractive, Vic thought, but not exactly full of life either.

'I usually have just a Cup-a-Soup and a crispbread but I can do you a fried egg if you like.'

Time for a basic lie: 'I had lunch at the canteen, thanks.'

'You don't mind if I carry on?'

'Not at all –'

'Only I've got another appointment at half past –'

Vic watched her move into the kitchen and switch the kettle on. She said, 'I can guess what you've come about.'

'If it's not all right, just say –'

'No, I'm glad you have. Just hang on a minute.'

When she came back she was stirring a blue mug with a Finn crispbread. She sat down holding the in both hands. 'He's been very cruel to me, V' still worn out, just totally worn out with it.' She bent her head over the mug, wings of dark hair hanging down each side, and breathed in the steam.

'What d'you think's wrong with him?'

She looked up. 'He said he hated me. He said he hated everything about me. What I did, what I said, how I looked. On and on and on, night after night. All sorts of things, wounding things, personal things – what a drag I was, how hopeless I was – in bed and out.' She flashed him a frank, defeated glance. 'How I wasn't a patch on her . . . How he wished it was me instead of her – oh God . . . Night after night . . . He wouldn't rest until he'd got me – I don't know – whimpering, begging him to stop, screaming at him, Leave me alone, please God, leave me alone . . .' She took a sip of soup; it left a mark on her upper lip. 'I was going suicidal, Vic, and all he did – all he did was smile at me. I can see his little girl's mouth doing it now –' She wiped her mouth with a yellow tissue from her sleeve. '*Jesus Christ, it wasn't my fucking fault she died, was it? Was it?*'

'No, Louise, it wasn't. She was in the wrong place at the wrong time, that's all.'

'Poor woman.'

'He ever hit you, Louise?'

'No. Said he wouldn't soil his hands on me.'

'Anything else?'

'He used to tell me how he'd shot those two – the ones that did it – and how he wished it was me. He was mental, Vic, and he was driving *me* mental –'

'And when you asked him to leave?'

Louise looked directly at him. 'He said he'd go when he'd finished with me.'

'And when was that?'

'Three, four weeks . . . You were his best mate, he used to think the sun shone out of your backside, what do *you* think's wrong with him? Why was he so – so fucking *vile* to me? I never did anything to hurt *him* –'

'I don't know. Maybe he felt smashed up wanted to smash somebody else up. You were there, you took him back, you were vulnerable. Who knows what goes on? I know I don't –'

She nodded, took a sip, then a good mouthful. To Vic it smelled of nothing but monosodium glutamate but it seemed to buck Louise up. 'But why – why did he find it . . . *so fucking enjoyable?*'

On the long drag through the traffic up to Clifton, Vic remembered what Cromer had said at the debriefing. They'd been looking at the video footage of Cromer bulked up in his black armoured vest walking out into the back garden of the house in Palmer Street. The bright flashes and flat sounds of two automatic weapons could be clearly seen and heard; Cromer had walked on into their fire without flinching. The commendation had said that Cromer had shown 'extraordinary bravery and devotion to duty in facing down two armed and violent criminals'. What the commendation did not say, but what the video footage indubitably showed, was that Cromer, after wounding and disarming both men, had bent over their bodies and deliberately shot each one in the back of the head. When Sam Richardson had asked him why the fuck he had jeopardised his whole career, Cromer had replied quietly and respectfully, 'At the time, sir, it seemed only fair.'

16

Before all four floors had been divided and sub-divided into rabbit-hutches, the house in St Pauls Road had been a spacious mid-Victorian semi: cream stucco lined to look like stone slabs; double bay windows; set between them a broad Georgian-panelled front door and a scallop-shell fanlight. Vic took the two steps up to the portico and looked down over the railings into the semi-basement. There were two windows and a separate glass-fronted side door; all three were blocked by heavy grey curtains. Vic had the choice of a tower of addressed plastic bell-pushes or a lacquered dolphin knocker.

He knocked twice; the door opened an inch or so. A penetrating male voice said, 'Look, I don't like you parking outside my house. It's my space and I have to pay for it, so I'm going to have to ask you to move –'

Vic held up his ID. 'Sergeant Hallam, Bristol CID, sir.'

The man, who looked to be in his early sixties, slim with slicked-back dyed black hair, a petulant mouth and a Mr Punch chin, took a step back. 'Oh –'

'Are you the landlord of this property, sir?'

'Yes, yes I am. Is anything wrong?'

'May I have your name please, sir?'

'Look, I'm allowed to park there, I got an invalid sticker for my knee as well as havin' to pay for bloody tenants –' The man's voice was becoming more Bristol by the second.

Vic said, 'It's nothing serious, Mr . . .?'

'Allington, Wally Allington.' He cocked his head to look past Vic to the houses opposite. 'Look, you'd better come in off the street – there's women over there wants to know all my business. Two of 'em got nothin' better to do all day –' Still glaring across the road, he moved back to let Vic through.

There was a shiny rubber plant on an umbrella stand in the black and white tiled hall and the usual boarding-house smell of polish, loo freshener and stale vegetables.

'Come in the kitchen, I was just havin' my bloody lunch.'

'I'm sorry about that, Mr Allington –'

'So am I.'

The kitchen still had its original diamond-paned built-in dresser with a white enamel fold-down work surface. Next to it was a Belfast sink and in the middle of the polished quarry-tiled floor stood four bentwood chairs around an enamel-topped table. Everything was old, well used but clean; lunch was a plate of ham, a tomato, a spoonful of Branston, a slice of brown bread from a wrapped loaf and a small bottle of imported Stella.

'Sit down if you like. I'm going to –'

'Thanks.'

He took a defiant swig of Stella. 'You want one?'

Vic shook his head. 'Not on duty, sir.'

'You don't mind if I start then?' He ate greedily: in Vic's experience nearly all men living on their own did. Every so often his eyes flicked up from his plate to Vic and back again.

'This is about a colleague of mine, Detective Sergeant Cromer.'

'He's not here, he's had to go away. On a job.'

'I know, we're working together.'

'Oh yes?'

'I had to come up here so he asked me to pick up a couple of things for him.'

'Such as?'

'His sports kit basically.'

'Yes, I noticed he left it all behind. He didn't tell me where he was going.' He looked up, hoping for an answer.

'All I can say is you forward any mail to the Bridewell.'

'So he told me. Anyway, he paid a month in advance, so I put a padlock on his door.'

'Very sensible, Mr Allington.'

'Just tell him when you see him if I don't hear from him within the month, the room'll be let. I'm not runnin' a bloody charity, police or no police. Do I make myself clear, Sergeant?'

'I'll tell him.'

'They do taekwondo where you are then?'

'There's a sports centre not far away.'

'Don't give much away do you?'

Vic smiled. 'Not paid to. So, just to get this straight, he's been here a month –'

'More or less –'

'And he's paid for one more?'

'When I asked him to, yes.' He pushed the plate away with his fingertips. 'Let me put it like this. This place is clean and not exorbitant. I usually have a few young men from the BBC down here on courses of one sort or another. Most of 'em but not all I regret to say are honest so having a copper on the premises is a bit of a plus. Also I don't give a bugger what they do in their spare time so long as they don't play their bloody music after midnight, they don't damage the furnishings and they don't throw up here there and everywhere. That answer your questions?'

'No women?'

'I used to, but apart from any other – considerations, shall we say? – I've cleaned out enough blocked lavatories for one lifetime, thank you very much. I won't have musicians either.' He stood up. 'I'll leave it up to you to reason why. Now if we can get on –'

Cromer's room was on the second floor facing the street. It shared half a window and a plasterboard partition with the room next door.

'His stuff's in the top of the wardrobe. In one of those awful plastic things. The boys in the club say your friend's pretty sharp. Might have made County if he'd stuck at it.'

Vic took the zippered suit-holder off the shelf. 'You ever do this, Mr Allington?'

'Why d'you ask?'

'I just wondered why you let the basement out to the club.'

'Yes, I did use to have a bit of a go but I started too late – it comes too damned hard on dodgy knees, you get to my age.'

Time to spread a little bullshit. 'You still look pretty fit.'

'I shall be seventy-three next birthday, if I'm spared.'

'You could have fooled me.'

'Oh yes?' Waiting for more as all these old guys did.

'I'd have said you were barely sixty, if that.'

Patting his flat stomach Mr Allington preened and smiled at himself in the wardrobe mirror. 'All down to a clean and healthy lifestyle, Sergeant.'

'You let the basement out for anything else?'

His smile soured and his chin jutted. 'Why? What's he been telling you?'

'This and that –'

'Listen Sergeant. We're all volunteers, we're all men over twenty-one and no money changes hands – I've been into it and we're perfectly legal – 'part from ought else we're not the only bloody rubber club in Bristol so why you should come pokin' your nose round here –'

'What did you say?'

'I've a good mind to chuck his stuff out on the street –'

'You said something about a rubber club –'

'Latex, to be precise – it's finer, more sensitive, more – erotic, if you really want to know –'

'You're not into S&M then?'

'For God's sake, Sergeant. What you think we are, perverts?'

17

Calder was in his underground office at the police morgue. A balding, thick-shouldered, ruddy-faced man in his shirtsleeves, he generated enough body heat in the chill atmosphere to mist up his titanium-rimmed spectacles. When Vic came in he had pushed them up on to his forehead and was using a scalpel to dissect a couple of pickled gherkins. In front of him lay a plate-sized open salt-beef sandwich, the meat carved at least as thick as the rye. He waved Vic to the chair opposite. 'You ever noticed how gherkins taste better sliced lengthways rather than chopped?'

'Can't say I have.'

'Try one.' Offering it on the point of the scalpel.

'Thanks.' Vic took it and bit into it. 'Wow –'

'What?'

'Hot –'

'Moroccan chum of mine makes 'em, steeps 'em in harissa and chilli vinegar, says all vegetables are better sliced.' He crunched into the gherkin. 'You said you wanted to see me.'

'Yeah. You remember Palmer Street?'

'Very busy night, as I recall –'

'Telling me.'

'Who are you interested in specifically, Vic?'

'Young woman called Opal Macalpine.'

Calder sliced off a couple of inches of salt beef and ate it off the scalpel. 'I don't eat the bread, caraway seeds stick in my teeth.'

'I'll have it if you like. I missed lunch –'

'Help yourself.' Calder chewed slowly, thinking back. 'Liver, kidney and spleen. Nine-millimetre Glock. Smack, smack. Waste of a perfectly healthy young woman.'

'She was Cromer's girl.'

'Lucky old him. Or not, as the case may be.'

'In this case, definitely not.'

'Meaning?'

'Not sure how to put this – I think he's gone funny on us.'

'He seemed well enough in control when I released the remains for cremation.'

'He was the only mourner, Mr Calder. He didn't tell me, he didn't tell her friends, he didn't tell the local funeral guy, Rufus –'

Calder nodded. 'I remember Rufus. Good man –'

'Rufus buried her friend Maelee and her stepfather Julius. Cromer had Opal cremated by the Co-op. I checked with them and they've got him down as the only mourner. And next of kin.'

'Was he?'

'Not really. Opal had a kid, a two-year-old, Esme –'

'Case of wishful thinking then? I mean, on Cromer's part –'

'Possibly – but then there's all this other weird stuff –'

'Such as?'

Vic told Calder about his visits to Louise and Wally Allington. Calder nodded and chewed: chewed and nodded. Vic ended by saying, 'Anyway, first thing set my alarm bells ringing was what he said about "Bringing the Gift" –'

'Jolly lot, our Korean friends.'

'What got me was the way he smiled afterwards.'

'Death –' Calder interrupted himself to bend the paper plate in half and drop it and its crumbs into the bin. Then he took his spectacles off his forehead, polished them on a hospital tissue and put them on. They were grey-tinted and made his eyes larger, bluer, madder. He steepled his fingers and pondered Vic like a man debating whether to entrust his wallet or his wife to a complete stranger. Vic wondered why the performance.

Maybe everybody in Calder's line of business was a bit dipped; perhaps you had to be to cut up dead people all day –

Calder said, 'You may think this a load of crap, Vic, but I've been doing this for twenty years now and there's always what I call that traffic-accident moment – when they look at you and you have to tell them exactly what's happened. You know?'

'Yeah.' Standing on the doorstep, saying to some young kid with jam all round his face *Hallo son is your mum in –*

'Death is a very rich meat, Vic,' said Calder. 'Too

rich for most people. They haven't got the stomach for it.' He gave Vic a half smile: 'You can say that's a load of old cobblers, but it's not like days gone by when the poor bloody women shoaled out kids and three-quarters of 'em died. People aren't used to that now. They expect more. Then suddenly – wham.' Calder wiped the palms of his hands on a bunch of tissues. 'There's nothing noble about grief, Vic, not in my experience. It's a trauma, a shock, a poison, it can leave you weak and debilitated, it can drive you raving mad – or you end up emotionally inert, a block of ice.'

Cromer's smile –

'Yeah, I see. Thanks anyway –'

As Vic stood up to go, Calder said, 'Oh, by the way – I got our Forensics to do some on-the-spot door-slam testing. I wouldn't say they made themselves very popular with the staff of the *Aware* – or with Mr Willoughby –'

'Why, what happened?'

'Apparently it sounded like a bloody bomb going off.'

'Yeah, it would, inside that hull.'

'What they found out, Vic, was that it didn't matter how you slammed those steels doors. Light or heavy, the result was much the same. Something to do with mass, inertia and the impact of the narrow leading edge. Even medium force was enough to burst a football. And a good heavy shove split a medicine ball wide open. After that they were more or less required to stop.'

'Can't say I'm surprised.'

'What it means, Vic, as I said to Willoughby on the phone, is that in the circumstances there was no question of excessive force being used by you or anybody else. Then I faxed him Forensic's figures.'

'And?'

'Let's just say he wasn't a very happy bunny.'

'Thanks Mr Calder.'

'Cheers Vic.'

18

The drawer was already open, the tray pulled out. The attendant drew the sheet back off the face and shoulders.

A young woman. Short fair hair. Wide cheekbones. Strong build.

The first body Cromer had seen since Opal's.

He remembered feeling nothing then; he felt nothing now.

Death was death and that was all.

Hang on to that –

He became aware of Willoughby – tall, pinstriped, swept-back silver hair – watching him. 'Sure you're up for this, Sergeant?'

Smiling back. 'I think so, sir.'

'You've seen all this before, of course?'

'Many times, Mr Willoughby.'

'Show Sergeant Cromer my Y-cut if you will, Stanley.'

The attendant turned down the sheet in folds.

Cromer swallowed: across the middle of the standard autopsy Y-cut from both nipples to the groin was a rough slash from stomach to lower bowel.

Willoughby said, 'Cause of death, burst condom or condoms. One can only hope they removed the rest of the heroin *after* she was dead.'

Cromer nodded.

'You will observe from the serrated edge of the wound that the tool used was almost certainly an electric jig saw. Black and Decker, Bosch, something like that.'

'Bastards.'

'This is what we're up against, Sergeant. I wanted you to see it for yourself.'

'Thank you, sir.'

'That's all, Stanley. Thank you.'

The attendant unfolded the sheet back over the body of the young woman, pausing to smooth her short fair hair before sliding the tray back into the wall and closing the insulated door.

Back in his office Willoughby took a file from his desk drawer. 'That's my report. I'd like you to fax it through to your Mr Calder, if you don't mind, and then return it to me.'

'As you wish – but shouldn't your secretary be doing this?'

'I think it best, Sergeant, that Mr Calder and myself deal with each other at arm's length via a known intermediary such as yourself, in order that no further misunderstandings can occur. Do I make myself clear?'

'Perfectly, Mr Willoughby.'

Calder had obviously managed to ruffle his feathers and rattle his cage.

Cromer read through the report in the car park. It was meticulous: so much so that Cromer guessed Willoughby intended it as a two-finger salute.

The body had been picked up by the *Old Harry*, a Weymouth boat longlining for bass in the race off Portland. It had been in the sea for not less than three days but had neither bloated nor floated due to the removal of almost all stomach content. The small amount that remained was reddish and shredded in colour and texture and indicated a hypothetical ingestion of beetroot, sauerkraut, and possibly, from small traces of pimento also found, goulash. This in turn could indicate a shipboard diet of either Balkan or East European origin. The body was found wrapped in black polythene bound with 5cm silver insulation tape. Contusions were found all over the torso, front and back, consistent in outline and position with regular beatings rather than falls. A fragment of surgical latex comprising the rim and part of a knot had been traced to a type of reusable condom manufactured by The London Rubber Company. This type of reusable was, according to the literature and reports of previous instances of either detection or death, common in the illegal importation of Class A narcotics: this was due to the supposed extra strength and protection against bursting this type of condom provided. A footnote added that abraded contusions in the region of the subject's solar plexus were consistent with a fall or blows from a heavily gloved fist or boot: any similar intervention may have caused such condoms to burst, but given the damaged condition of the skin and severed flesh in the immediate area, any such first cause must remain purely conjectural.

Cromer laid the report aside and recalled her calm, pale face. A cold anger welled up in him. He felt months of inertia – inertia that he had proudly assumed was self-control – being swept away like matchwood. He was going to get these bastards and make them pay for what they had done to this young woman.

It was, after all, only fair.

19

Relieved that Calder had got him off the hook, Vic drove down to Financial Enquires in the Bridewell. A maze of security checks later, Doochy's bank faxed through the transaction details on his Mastercard.

One look was enough: at the start of the thirty-day period Doochy's credit limit stood at well over three grand. There were three or four fifty-quid withdrawals, weekly payments to Bushells Wines, and over the last fortnight ten maximum cash withdrawals of three hundred quid a time.

Somebody had cleaned out Doochy's Mastercard.

Vic took the A37 south and reached Weymouth about six. Bushells Wines was a corner shop between two run-down terraced streets on the east side of town. He walked in, checked the black and white CCTV screen and pretended to look through the Australian reds while two fifteen-year-olds put the contents of their pockets together for a flagon of White Lightning. The assistant, a pasty-faced young woman name-tagged Meryl, counted every coin twice, wrapped the bottle in green tissue, slipped it in a white plastic bag and told the two youths not to drink it outside. She looked scarcely older than they did.

When they left, Vic laid his ID on the counter. 'Hallo, Meryl, been working here long?'

She glanced at his ID, looked up dead-eyed. 'I went to Weymuff College with them two. They're over eighteen –'

'I doubt it, but that's not why I'm here.'

'Makes a bloody change then.'

Vic pulled the Bushells and Mastercard receipts out of his pocketbook. 'I want you to have a look at these for me, see if you remember serving this customer.'

'Why?' Hard as nails –

'Because I'm asking you to.'

'They in bother then?'

'Let's just say it's a friend of mine.'

'I ain't seen you round here before.'

'No you haven't, and you don't want to see me round here again, do you?'

A couldn't-give-a-fuck shrug. 'Please yourself.'

Vic smiled and looked round the shop. 'Can't be easy to get a job round here.'

'Whassat supposed to mean?'

'It means I want you to look at the receipts, Meryl. Bacardi, Pepsi six-pack, two hundred Camel Lights. The same order on the same day, once a week for the last month or so. If you know, you can tell me, can't you? If you don't –'

'Wha'?' Letting her mouth hang open.

'Well, Meryl, I'll have to ask the manager, won't I?'

She picked up the receipts, took as long as she could going through them. Then, sullen as hell: 'Could be Allie.'

'Allie?'

'Little bloke.' She put her hand level with her breasts. 'Comes up to about here. Goin' a bit thin on top.'

'He live round here?'

'Yeah somewhere.' The dead-eyed look. 'I only bin 'ere free weeks.'

'He got another name?' Vic pointed at the signatures. 'Duchene possibly?'

'I dunno do I? All I know he's Allie the Scouser, from the Verne. He gets fags and stuff for one a the blokes in there. Anyfin' else you wanna know?'

'Are these his signatures?'

'I dunno.'

'You served him, Meryl. Have another look, will you?'

'Could be. Serves all sorts a people, dun I?'

'Thank you, Meryl. You've been most kind.'

As the doorbell jangled behind him: 'Eff off, wanka.'

A mobile phone call to the Verne and Vic had the address. He rang the bell on a neat terrace house a couple of hundred yards down the slope from Bushells Wines. Unlike the others it had a red Cardinal-polished front step and the patterned net curtains were clean. A little old lady with a bent back opened the door but kept the chain on. 'Who is it?'

'My name's Vic, I used to work with Allie on the *Aware*.'

'Just a minute. I'll tell him.'

Vic heard her slippers shuffle away, and her thin voice calling up the stairs: 'Allie! A man called Vic, from work –'

'All right Mam, I'll gerrit –'

The feet shuffled back. Because she couldn't lift her head very far, Vic found himself looking down on the top of her scalp. It was pink under sparse white hair. 'He's on his computer. I'm his mother.'

'Thanks very much, Mrs Sullivan. Sorry to trouble you.'

'I'll let Allie do the chain if you don't mind. It's a bit high up and fiddly for me –' Feet shuffling away again, the clack of a loose tile, a door opening, the sound of *The Simpsons* on telly – then Allie's thin jockey's face at the door.

''Allo Vic –' Sounding surprised.

'Can I have a word?'

'Yeah, yeah, yeah. Sure.' Rattling the chain out of its slot, grinning, but nervous. 'You've met me mam, then – she can't gerrabout much but she likes to know what's goin' on, know what I mean?'

Inside the tiled hall there was a narrow table with a china figure of Jesus, his hand raised in benediction over a gold-rimmed candleholder.

'Come on up, Vic – we'll leave Mam to watch telly –'

Allie's room was at the front. There was an old wooden bed with a shiny blue and gold Virgin in Glory above it, a wardrobe and a computer on a black Argos work-station. Tropical fish glooped and bleeped across the screen. 'I'll just turn this off.' As Allie sat at the keyboard to shut down Windows 98, Vic wondered how Allie's mother would cope without her son.

Unless there was another way . . .

'How you been doin' then Vic? Eh? Y'all right?'

'It's not good news, Allie.'

Allie nodded and slumped forward on the typing chair, his wrists dangling between his knees. 'No, I didn' think it was. Soon as I heard it was you, like, I knew –'

'Why did you do it, Allie?'

The daft silly grin of small-time villains every-where. As if you'd made the rules so it was your fault they'd broken them. 'I don' know Vic, you tell me.'

'Doochy know you were forging his signature?'

'Oh yeah. Yeah – that was the whole idea, Vic. So I could get his snouts and his Bacardi an' coke, like. Poor kid hadden got owt else, had he?'

'Apart from the grass, no.'

Another weak grin. 'Yeah, that an' all – but they're all doin' it, Vic, all the staff, they're all in on it. Every-where, not just the *Aware* – friggin' lid would blow off the whole friggin' Verne without the cons got their friggin' smoko –'

'What – fifty quid a week for home-grown?'

'Yeah, well –'

'Well what?'

'Look, Vic – well, Doochy was, you know, he was a black kiddie, wadden he? Brought up on it, been smokin' the old ganja since he was a kid, like. An' afta, you know, afta all that when he 'ad that seein'-to, he said it was better for the pain, like, better than any amount a paracodeine we could give him. That kinda pain lasts, you know, Vic. Gets in all your muscles an' lasts for weeks, like you got friggin' permanent bloody flu. Old Doochy was a hard case all right but he wadden that hard – said the grass made him feel better –'

'You used to talk to him didn't you?'

'Old Doochy? Yeah, we 'ad the odd natter. Before he had his seein'-to and you turned up, no bugger else to talk to, was there? I use ta take him his tea mornin' and afternoon – he use ta stick three sugars in it – I use ta say he'd rot his teeth out but they don't seem to, do they, these black kiddies?'

'What did you talk about, Allie?'

'Oh y'know, this an' that. Liverpool an' that – he knew the Pool well, bein' in the Merch –'

'He ever say anything about getting out, what he was going to do?'

'Oh Christ yes, all the time –'

'What'd he say?'

'Said as soon as he got his money he was gettin' the first boat back to St Lucia an' this friggin' white-man cat-piss weather wouldn' see him no more –'

'What money?'

'Said he'd got a "piece a bizniss" waitin' on him the day he got out –'

'"A piece of bizniss"?'

'He always called it that – I use ta pull his leg, like. Hallo Dooch, what bizniss we on today, got your gee-gees picked out yet? I'd put his bets on for him of a lunchtime –'

'I see.'

'Anythin' to pass the time, like – because as you know yourself Vic, time drags like bloody lead in there –'

'He ever say what sort of business?'

'He didn' have to did he? What he was in for, wadden it?'

'Drugs?'

'Yeah.' Allie grinned. 'He use to say me an' him was in the same game – pharmaceuticals –'

'Heroin, cocaine, or what?'

'All sorts – you must a seen his record Vic – long as both friggin' arms –'

'Yeah. He ever mention "smack for crack"?'

Allie straightened up and folded his arms. 'Eh?'

'He ever mention his "Big Idea"?'

Frowning now, trying to look serious, helpful. 'No, not as I recall. Why, somethin' goin' on is there?'

'You were with him straight after he got done over. What was he like – he talk at all?'

'Oh yeah, but you know, he was mitherin', like, wanderin'. They had him on morphine, see. A lorra blokes go on about their mothers an' that – but Doochy had that funny lingo –'

'Patois?'

'Yeah, that's it –'

'So nothing about smack for crack?'

The arms still folded. 'Not to my knowledge, no.'

'He ever talk about money?'

'Oh yeah.' Looking relieved. 'He was always on about makin' his stash, yeah. Use ta say he was goin' home like a big-up –'

'He ever say how?'

'Only this "piece of bizniss" he had goin' –'

'You ever tell anybody else? The prison officers?'

'No friggin' fear – nothin' to do with me, was it? I ain't no friggin' mouth-artist Vic – too dangerous round here. The blacks and these asylum guys they all got shivs an' spikes and sharped-up six-inch nails –'

'You ever talk to any of them?'

'I do the medication for the ones in solitary. Hardly any of 'em speaks English but they're all on the rob for friggin' headache pills –'

'Any money in it?'

'You daren't Vic, not on solitary.'

'You think Doochy ever told anybody else?'

'Be a right friggin' clown, wouldn' he?'

'Yeah, I suppose.'

Allie looked round the room, leaned forward. 'Somebody musta known somethin' Vic, or he wouldna got duffed up, would he? Or topped –'

Vic nodded, as if conceding the issue. 'That's a point –'

'All he use ta tell me how he was gonna walk down that gangplank with a big sack a money and prezzies over his shoulder. Man, he use ta say, I'm gonna be the first black mutha Father Christmas them folks ever seen. "Heh-heh-heh" he'd go, "heh-heh-heh –" '

'This was before he got done over?'

Relaxing now. 'Yeah, right.'

Time to start twisting the knife: 'So you didn't feel too bad about taking fifty quid a week off him for grass?'

'Not if it made him feel better –'

'Fifty quid a week better?'

'Yeah, well I had to take a bit for me trouble, didn' I? For the risk, like.'

'I see.'

'Look Vic, you hadden been there long enough to know, but every so often the screws 'ave a friggin' blitz on it – you're found carryin', you're out, sunshine. Up the road, lick 'em an' stick 'em, no friggin' comebacks and no chance of another job nowhere –'

'So you took the fifty for the grass out in cash?'

'Dealers round 'ere ain't gonna take a friggin' cheque, are they? Or a friggin' credit card.'

Vic took the folded fax out of his pocketbook and smoothed it out in front of Allie. 'I hear what you're saying, Allie, but by the end, you weren't taking fifty out, were you? You were going for the full whack, three hundred a time, practically every fucking day. Weren't you?'

Allie's face crumpled: he started to look like his mother. 'It was too friggin' easy –'

'What about the bank?'

'I 'ad the statements and that redirected here. Doochy didn' mind – they'd only get opened in the Verne.' An apologetic grin 'Anyway they asked me to phone 'em – you know, all these three hundreds – they got fellers checkin' that sort a thing.'

'Yeah, I know.'

'I didn'. Nearly shat meself –'

'What did you do?'

'Phoned 'em didn't I? Had to –'

'Said you were Doochy?'

'Yeah.'

'They want proof of identity?'

'Yeah. His mother's maiden name.'

'And you knew it?'

Allie nodded. 'Evangeline Duchene – wasn't married, see.'

'How?'

'I asked Doochy, didn' I? Before I phoned back. Everybody likes goin' on about their fam'ly, Vic, where they come from. Specially in there. All they got left, some of 'em.'

'Must've made you feel a right shit.'

'Oh yeah.' The weak grin. 'Well I am, arn' I? The

thing is Vic, you get so far in you can't stop – you know?'

'Yeah. How about the accent?'

'No problem. A lorra black blokes have Liverpool accents.'

'And the money?'

'I said I was buyin' a car for three grand and the feller wanted cash.'

'Then what?'

'I couldn' believe it –'

'What?'

'Friggin' bank only offered me a four-grand loan, didn' they? Said it'd be cheaper than Mastercard.' Shaking his head. 'Friggin' banks, eh? Worst a the friggin' lot.'

'You take it?'

Allie turned the key in the underslung drawer of the work station, took out a fat A4 envelope and held it out to Vic. 'I was goin' to. Then you friggin' well turn up.'

Vic took the envelope. 'Thanks. Where's the rest of the money, Allie?'

Allie leaned back and stared at the blue and gold Virgin in Glory above his bed. 'Down the bookies – three an' half friggin' grand, an' Ladbrokes got the friggin' lot . . . I thought, you know, one half-decent win an' I could see him right, put us all back square . . .' His voice trailed off.

Vic waited. Allie put his head in his hands and stared at the floor. From what Vic could see of his face, his mouth seemed to be moving now and then.

Maybe he was praying; maybe it was just the same old bullshit – maybe there wasn't any difference –

His head lifted and he looked Vic in the eye. 'You know what, Vic? I'm glad it's out, it's been drivin' me round the bend, I've been goin' fuckin' mad here . . . What d'you think'll happen, Vic?'

Now – lay it on him. Hard.

'You could be looking at up to five years, Allie. And not in the fucking Verne either. Banks go for the max on credit fraud, and because you conned a sick and helpless man you'll get no sympathy from the jury.'

'Oh shit. Wharram I gonna tell me mam?'

'I don't know.'

'Who's gonna look after her?'

'If she can't look after herself, they'll have to put her in a home. You knew that, didn't you?'

Allie's eyes began to water. 'Oh Christ, Vic, it'll kill her.'

Vic watched the tears running down into the creases on Allie's cheeks. First you screwed the bloke down to his knees, then you pretended to help him back up again . . .

He said, 'You know Doochy had a wife and kids?'

'Yeah yeah yeah, I know . . . Oh shit – wharram I gonna do, Vic?'

'You could always take your own loan out for a change.'

'Wha'?'

'Take out a loan and pay off the credit card.'

'That'd be nigh on four grand –'

'Yeah. Price of freedom, Allie.'

'Eh?'

'You heard me.'

'You mean you're not bangin' me up? I'm not goin' down?'

'I can guarantee you won't. So long as you pay back the money, nobody else'll know.' Vic held his hand out. 'I'll take his card, though.'

Allie pulled his wallet from his back pocket, slipped out Doochy's Mastercard. 'Here, 'ave it. Poor old Doochy –'

'Yeah, poor old Doochy.'

A hope-against-hope grin: 'That the end of it then?'

'What do you think?'

'Nothin' for nothin' in this world, is there?'

'That's right, Allie.'

'Oh fuck, Vic, why did he 'ave to go an' fuckin' die?'

'That's what we're going to find out. You and me.'

'That the deal?'

'That's the deal.'

'How?'

'There's an older guy in there, grey-haired, not in solitary, speaks reasonable English. He seems more educated than the rest, advises 'em, tells 'em what to do. Told 'em what to put on their statements. Bit of a barrack-room lawyer.'

'Oh yeah. Edi. Thickset feller.'

'That's him. Anyway, talk to him. That's what you're good at, Allie. Talking to people, conning the poor bastards . . . Aren't you?' Allie looking at him, saying nothing. 'What you do is get close to him, then through him to the others. Booze, fags, all that shit you pulled on Doochy. Then you let on you know something about this smack-for-crack thing. Tell 'em Doochy told you – not much, just this and that. Enough to show you're interested – let 'em get the idea for the right sort of money you could be willing to help –'

'They'll fuckin' kill me –'

'No they won't – they got people outside, Allie, people they need to contact. They need in on this deal, Allie – that's why they did Doochy –'

'Yeah, why they'll do me an' all –'

'Not if you offer to take out messages, letters, bring in a mobile, fetch and carry. That's where they're fucked at the moment – that's what they *need*. Just don't ask for too much. You serve their purpose, they stay safe inside, everybody's happy.'

'You reckon?'

'They've already got you down as a good bloke, Allie.' Taking a risk, Vic leaned forward, patted him on the knee. 'Well, you are, aren't you? It's in your nature.' Smiling at him now, pretending to be kind –

Allie, frowning, looking confused – as he was meant to be . . . 'Gorra do somethin' 'aven' ya? Relieve the fuckin' tedium –'

Now stick it to him –

'Yeah – you'd do anything for anybody, wouldn't you? Specially when it's that or jail. That and all the rest of it.' Vic waited for it to sink in.

'Then what?'

'Then anything they tell you, you tell me. Fair enough?'

Allie nodded acceptance. 'Yeah. Fair enough.'

Vic left Allie in his bedroom and walked out of the house alone. Allie's mother was still watching *The Simpsons*. He was careful not to tread on her red Cardinal-polished step.

He sat in the diesel Cavalier outside Bushells Wines, turned on the ignition and waited for the orange glow-plug indicator to cut out.

Thing was, even if you won you felt fucking dirty.

20

'You ever been rabbiting, John?'

'I've been lamping. We had this Land-Rover with a row of headlights on the roof. Took it down Sedgemoor –'

'No, this is rabbiting with rathounds – half a dozen Jack Russells in the boot of an old banger.'

'No, can't say I have. Why?'

They had started at half eight; it was now ten and they were having a fag-and-coffee break. Vic and Cromer were spread out along both arms of the horseshoe banquette in Cromer's mobile home and the beer-ringed coffee table between them was piled with papers and print-outs from Vic's PC and Cromer's brand-new laptop. The sun shone directly through the smoked Plexiglass window and filled the room with dust-laden lager-coloured light.

Vic said, 'What you do is, you find a warren, stop up all the holes but two. You net the downwind one and put the Jacks in upwind. You can use old oily rags soaked in pink diesel as well but most farmers are too fucking mean and it doesn't do the dogs a lot of good either –'

'Then what?'

'Well, after a lot of yapping and screaming, you've got a net full of rabbits – the dogs get one and you break the necks of the rest.'

'Sounds like good clean fun.'

'Better than mixy, John.'

'What's this to do with the price of fish?'

'So far, on this job, it looks as if we've stopped up all the holes. All the ones we know about anyway.'

'And you reckon it's time to send the dogs in?'

'No, not yet. Even if Doochy hadn't got done over he still wouldn't have got out before next week. And even though he told matey here . . .' Vic fished a copy of his interview with Allie from the pile on the table: 'Even though he told Allie he'd got this "piece of bizniss" waiting for him as soon as he got out, we all know life doesn't work out like that –'

'There's the fuck-up factor to take into account –'

'Exactly.'

'So we don't send the dogs in?'

'We're the dogs, kiddo.'

'What I was thinking –'

'So what we do is get a report off to Sam Richardson –'

'By "we" you mean me?'

'You're the one with the fancy laptop, John.'

'Oh yeah. Hoo-fucking-ray –'

'Look, all we do is put my floppy in with your floppy –'

'Fucking obscene for a start –'

'– cut and paste 'em together, indicate further action required, email Sam Richardson plus attachments and let him worry about it.'

'Then what?'

'We go fishing.'

Now there was some routine stuff to deal with, Vic was starting to feel better about Cromer: He was getting back up to speed, he'd stopped nitpicking, and that weird fucking edginess seemed to have been replaced with something more like grim enthusiasm. Vic put it down to his meeting with Willoughby and his follow-up inquiries concerning the young woman's body at Police HQ Winfrith and Portland Coastguard. Cromer had found something new to get his teeth into. It was what happened when you were a cop: one case wiped out the one before and your batteries got a big recharge. It had happened to Vic often enough: there was always a down after a case and the less you had to do the more manky and morose you felt. It was only when you were lying shot up in a hospital bed – or in Cromer's case, moping around and taking it out on Louise – that you felt like saying fuck it, I quit. The simple fact there was a job on got your brain up and your blood pumping –

What Cromer had said at half past eight that morning was, 'Something happened when I saw how they'd cut up that poor cow – all for fucking *money*, Vic –'

'Yeah –'

'I really want to get these fuckers –'

'Good for you –'

Then grinning: 'When I come down here you must've thought I was a right moody old queen –'

'Not old, John.'

'Fuck off, Hallam –'

It looked like Sam was right: Work. Cures everything.

By midday they had cut and pasted their separate reports into a single file and attached FURTHER ACTIONS REQUIRED:

```
1. JULIAN DUCHENE (DOOCHY)
SEE: REPORTS 1-3 (ASSAULT/
INTERVIEWS/DEATH) DS HALLAM.
Witness now deceased. Prisoner on
HMP AWARE.
Claimed to have originated/set up
imminent "SMACK FOR CRACK" opera-
tion, a new exchange/barter method
of trading HEROIN/COCAINE. Last
words: "A PIPE". Repeated several
times.
So far no perceived relevance.
Possible patois?
ACTION: DET CH SUP RICHARDSON>ROYAL
ST LUCIA CONSTABULARY.


2. ALASTAIR SULLIVAN
SEE REPORT 4 DS HALLAM.
Witness is male nurse on HMP AWARE.
```

Has been milking DUCHENE's Mastercard. Has agreed to restore funds in return for immunity from prosecution. As a result has been persuaded to infiltrate suspects on HMP AWARE re their attempts to muscle in on forthcoming "SMACK FOR CRACK" operation. Anything further known?
ACTION: DET CH SUP RICHARDSON>DRUG SQUADS UK>INTERPOL

3. RAMIZ SHEHU
SEE STATEMENT 'A' DS HALLAM
Witness now deceased. Prisoner on HMP AWARE.
Deceased caused death of DUCHENE, attempted murder DS HALLAM. Own death due to murder attempt.
Ex-member SIGURIMI, Albanian State Security.
Known State assassination squad member. Convictions, armed robbery, drugs. Had associates both inside and outside HMP AWARE. Associates outside tried to contact/threaten DS HALLAM: see photograph/'I SHAL RITERN' message attached.
Further knowledge of outside associates' links with inside associates required.
ACTION: DET CH SUP RICHARDSON>DRUG SQUADS>INTERPOL

4. UNKNOWN WOMAN #09
SEE REPORTS 1-3 (AUTOPSY/WINFRITH
HQ/COASTGUARD) DS CROMER
Body found in sea end March this
year. Young woman, 18-24, possible
East European origin, possible
victim vice/drug trafficking. Death
due to burst condom/s full of heroin.
Stomach sawn open to retrieve rest of
heroin. Copy of autopsy report
enclosed. Investigation at Police HQ
Winfrith revealed Immigration Vice
Unit closed down due to lack of
funding. Coastguard have no March
record of freighters outside mid-
Channel separation lanes; no recent
evidence of vice/drug trafficking
via smaller vessels, e.g. trawlers,
yachts etc.
ACTION: DET CH SUP RICHARDSON> DRUG
AND VICE SQUADS> IMMIGRATION>
CUSTOMS & EXCISE.

Vic watched Cromer print and send the last couple
of pages: 'That should give old Sam something to
think about. Right, let's get down to the boat – got
any cold beer?'

'Couple of four-packs in the fridge.'

'What of?'

'Budvar.'

'Couldn't be better. Joe's favourite –'

'Yeah,' said Cromer. 'And mine.'

Joe was in *Rob Roy*'s wheelhouse with a heavy-shouldered, big-bellied guy in a leather jacket and a black and green tartan shirt. Joe was talking him through the hand controls: twin throttles, forward/reverse, trim tabs and propeller pitch. The other guy was nodding but seemed more interested in playing with the wheel and adjusting the pump-up seat. When he came out on deck Vic saw he had a mass of black and grey permed hair like an eighties footballer – just short of a mullet – and a coarse, once-handsome face with the watery eyes and red apple-cheeks of the cider drinker.

Scrump Giffen –

'Oh shit, John –'

'What?'

'I forgot – Joe's hiring the boat out –'

Cromer hoiked up the two four-packs: 'Saves my beer –'

'Hang on a minute.'

Joe came out on deck. 'All right Vic?'

'Just wondered if you were going out at all.'

Joe hesitated, then turned to Scrump: 'You met my partner Vic, Roger?'

'Seen him about.' A deep, grudging voice, then, nodding at Cromer's back. 'Who's the nipper?'

Vic said, 'Friend of mine, name's John.'

'That beer he's carryin'?'

Cromer turned round. 'What's it look like?'

Oh Christ, John –

Vic said, 'We were thinking about going mackerelling –'

'Yeah, well,' said Joe. 'Thing is, Roger here's thinking about hiring the boat –'

'I know,' said Vic. 'I forgot –'

'I was just taking him out for half an hour, show him the ropes.' Joe looked at Scrump. 'Up to you, Roger.'

'Fine bloody start this is . . .' Then, seeming to relent: 'I tell you what, son –'

'You talking to me?'

For fuck sake, John –

'I tell you what – you get over the Slipway Stores, pick up a couple of flagons of Old Dog, we'll call it a deal.'

Cromer said, 'What's Old Dog?'

'Old Dog Rough, my son. Cider.'

Vic pulled out a tenner. 'Here you are, John.'

Cromer, putting the four-packs on the quay, muttering to Vic: 'This a good idea?'

'Find out, won't we?'

While Cromer was away, Joe started the engine. Scrump peered over the stern and shook his head at the burst of black diesel smoke. 'Don' go a lot on them injectors, Joe.'

'Always the same on start-up, Roger.'

'Like a bloody old donkey engine –'

Joe pulled both throttles back. A cloud of blue smoke enveloped the stern. 'That any better, Roger?'

Cromer came back with two plastic bottles of cloudy yellow liquid. The label showed a mangy but grinning three-legged dog. Vic said, 'Tell you what John – you get the booze on and I'll cast off.'

Vic threw Scrump the stern line and held the boat on the bow, one turn round the bollard, while Joe swung the stern out. As Vic stepped down on to the foredeck and dropped the line over the alloy cleat, he heard Cromer say, 'Where we going anyway?'

Joe said, 'Up Eype and on to St Gabriel's see if there's any bass running.'

'Up where?'

'Eype, end of the next headland along.'

'"Eep"?' said Cromer. 'I always thought that was "Ipe" –'

Scrump said, 'Typical bloody grockle –'

Joe said, 'A lot of holidaymakers call it "Ipe", John, but we're going up Eype –'

Vic picked up the boat hook, ready to fend off, but there was no need: Joe backed *Rob Roy* smoothly out into mid-channel and slipped her into forward. As they eased along the port side of the Cut, Vic stowed the boat hook under the rubber bungee cords on top of the cabin.

'Up Eep' . . .

'Up Ipe' . . .

. . . 'A pipe'?

I owe you one, Doochy –

21

Once they were out of range of the rod-fishermen making casts off the harbour entrance, Vic dug a couple of hand-lines out of the tackle box. When they had untangled the hooks and feathers from the rectangular wooden hand-reels he and Cromer stood in the open stern and started to troll for mackerel. 'All you do, John, is make sure the trace is running free –'

'What's the trace?'

'The bit with the feathers and the hooks on . . . Stand well to one side so you don't foul the props, let out twenty, thirty yards to clear the wake and then heave the line slowly forward and back – as if you were using a scythe –'

'Why?'

'It makes the mackerel think the feathers are fish – small stuff like whitebait –'

'Yeah, but why go for a bunch of manky old feathers?'

'You ever scuba'd?'

'Yeah –'

'Well, when you look up at the surface from below it's all silvery, like a mirror. To the mackerel the feathers look like flittery black shadows – fish.'

Cromer watched Vic heave the hand-line forward and let it trail back: 'You really get off on this stuff, don't you?'

'Peace of mind, John. You ought to try it.' He held the line between thumb and two fingers, feeling for a bite. 'Every so often you get something to eat as well –'

Vic left Cromer on the stern and moved up towards the wheelhouse.

Scrump was saying, 'How you gettin' on with the 'ouse then Joe? You finished or you goin' on throwin' money at 'er for ever?'

'Don't talk to me about money, Roger.'

'Can't be that bad, big 'ouse, boat like this –'

'Worse than bad – got the fucking bank at my fucking throat. Wouldn' be renting out to you otherwise, would I?'

'No need to be like that – all that stuff I pushed your way when I was on the reclamation –'

'On the nick, more like.'

'Saved you thousands on them roof beams alone –'

'Yeah. Now they're sending a bloke round to see if they got the worm. Trying to pull false pretences –'

'Sounds like the old repo gag to me, Joe.'

'How the fuck do you know?'

'Been there, 'aven' I? You wanna do what I did.'

'What's that?'

'Go through the 'oop. Get made bankrupt. They can't take a man's 'ouse, Joe.'

'Oh yes they fucking can. And the fucking boat –'

'Play your cards right, I'll take it off your hands –'

'You haven't got any money –'

'I might 'ave. Fact, I *will* have –'

'Not out of duff fucking outboards you won't.'

'Ain't talking about that, my friend –'

'What then?'

Scrump tapped the side of his nose. 'Say nothin', that's me.'

'You'll only piss it up the wall, Roger.'

'You got to 'ave it to piss it, kid.'

'True –'

'You gonna drive us all the way out and back? Thought I was 'elping you out by takin' her on for a couple of weeks –'

'Hang on a minute –' Joe checked the heading and the distance off, throttled back and handed the wheel over to Scrump.

The first thing he did was slam both throttles wide open, bang the boat up on to the plane and then jam the wheel hard over. The *Rob Roy* heeled into a lee-rail-under curve flinging them and everything else across the deck. Engine screaming, props thrashing out rooster-tails of spray, the *Rob Roy* smashed into its own wash and slewed sideways. Cromer, who was on the downside of the turn, was hanging on to the sternpost, head and chest over the side. Thrown back along the deck, Vic heard Joe shout, 'Christ sake shut the fucking throttles!'

As he did so, Scrump said, 'Thought I'd see what she'd do –'

With both throttles down, the *Rob Roy* stopped dead and lay rocking in the seethed-up chop. Vic said, 'You all right John?'

Cromer hauled himself back inboard and looked at his right hand. The orange propylene twine had tightened and left a dark red weal across his palm. His eyes lasered into Scrump's back. 'I'll have that cunt –'

'Steady on John.'

'Don't worry Vic. I don't mean now –'

Vic saw Joe click the wheelhouse door shut. Joe's look: *Man's a prat but I need the money* . . .

Vic said, 'You didn't go a lot on him from the start.'

'Calling me nipper, kid. Do this, do that, fetch my fucking cider –'

'It's more than that, John.'

Cromer stared at him. 'How d'you know?'

Vic shrugged.

Cromer said, 'Soon as I saw him –'

'What?'

'He reminded me . . . Fat-gutted twat . . .'

The two hand-reels were skipping and clattering about in the scuppers. Practically all the twine had run off both of them. Vic put his foot on one, picked up the other and started to wind back on to the reel. 'Reminded you of what?'

'You know those two guys in Palmer Street? One of 'em had hair like that –'

'What – permed?'

'Could've been. I don't know. Anyway it was right down the back of his neck and when I put the gun in, and offed him, I could smell his hair, singeing.'

Vic said, 'Sounds if you're still having nightmares –'

'No, Vic, I never dream.'

I bet you don't.

When Vic had reeled both lines in, there were two mackerel on one, four on the other. Vic looked round for the wood-and-iron priest they used to knock fish on the head. It had gone: washed down the scuppers into the sea. He thought about showing Cromer how to get the hooks out but decided he would only get himself more lacerated. Instead, Vic held each still-jerking fish firmly behind the gills, unhooked them, and threw them in the black rubber bait-bucket.

The wheelhouse door banged open and Scrump squeezed himself out. 'You can't leave 'em like that –'

'Priest's gone –'

'Cruelty to fish –' With a grunt Scrump bent his belly over the bait-bucket and pulled out a mackerel. He held it in his left hand, thrust his right forefinger into its gasping mouth, put his thumb on top of its head, and levered upwards. A soft crunchy snick as its spine broke and Scrump tossed its already stiff body back in the bucket. 'There y'are, quick and merciful. You want to 'ave a go, young 'un, learn summat useful for once?'

'No thanks.'

Scrump grunted and picked up another. 'More fool

you.' Snap went its spine. He turned to Vic. 'Way the real fishermen do it. Better'n any priest.' He picked up both flagons from the scuppers and squeezed himself sideways back into the wheelhouse.

Joe took them in slowly towards Eype. A narrow stream bordered by mud and glistening blue lias straggled across the shell-and-pebble beach. Behind it, an unsurfaced path climbed upwards, became a gravelled single track and led off into a car park. Above it, on the sheep-cropped hill, stood a white-painted clapboard chalet.

Cromer said, 'Is that it – Eype?'

'This is Eype Mouth. Eype Village is up the track, John. You can't see it from here.'

Joe was holding the boat head to sea. There was hardly any swell and from the stern you could see the shell-and-shingle bottom. It looked only inches away from the slow-churning props but was, Vic guessed, about half a metre.

Scrump leaned back against the wheelhouse door and lowered the plastic flagon. 'This as close as you can get, Joe?'

'It is without grounding. Dries out at low water.'

'What's the bottom like?'

'Clean.'

Cromer said, 'You can see it from here.'

'Be bloody blind not to.' Scrump took another swig of Old Dog, turned back to Joe. 'Right. Let's have a look at St Gabriel's.'

*

Joe took the boat a quarter of a mile out and put the fish finder on. The six-inch screen showed the occasional trace of mackerel or pollock but nothing larger. Vic gutted one of the mackerel and cut it into four chunks. Scrump stuck his head out of the wheelhouse. 'No point in guttin' 'em. Blood's what they silvery things go for.'

Vic said, 'Is that a fact?'

Joe said, 'Roger's right, Vic.'

Cromer said, 'He always is, isn' he?'

Scrump grinned and tipped up his flagon. 'You young bugger.'

It was about four miles from Eype Mouth to St Gabriel's. While Joe showed Scrump how to set up the GPS satnav and auto pilot Vic baited up a couple of boat rods for bass.

Cromer said, 'What's he talking about, "silvery things"?'

'What the locals call salmon and sea trout. You're not supposed to catch 'em at sea –'

'Why not?'

'DEFRA says it stops them going upriver to spawn. Fishermen say it stops the rich buggers catching 'em in the rivers.'

'Same old story then – one law for the rich, another for the poor.'

'Same old socialist crap more like. Fishermen aren't poor, they're just fucking greedy – you can get thirty or forty quid or more off a restaurant for a good wild salmon.'

'Jesus. You think we'll get any?'

'Unlikely.'

'Pity.'

'If we do and you get caught with a couple in a wet sack just swear blind somebody told you they were haddock.'

As they passed well outside the sandstone-topped bulk of Golden Cap, Scrump stuck his head out again: 'Highest cliff in the south of England, my son –'

Cromer said, 'How high's that then?'

'Six hundred an' seventeen feet to the trig point.'

'I thought you might know.'

Joe took the boat off auto pilot and headed cautiously out round the overfalls off St Gabriel's Ledge.

Vic said, 'All right to cast, Joe?'

'Hang on a minute. I want to show Roger something.'

As they came level with the flat semi-submerged rock where St Gabriel's footpath ended, the satnav pinged out the waypoint Joe had entered. 'There you are Roger, right on the nose.'

'Fuck me –'

'Accurate to within three metres, day or night, auto pilot on or off.'

'That's some piece a fuckin' kit, Joe . . . Still won't get us ashore though, will it?'

'You'd need the dinghy for that. And flat calm.'

For the next hour they fished the small choppy race

between St Gabriel's Ledge and the rocks of the Western Patches off the Cap. They had a couple of bites and Cromer saw the silver twist of a six-pound bass leaping and throwing his line, but they caught nothing.

Back in the cool of the flagstoned Harbour Bar, Vic said, 'Well John, we might have come back empty-handed, but we found out a couple of things.'

Cromer looked at the weal on his right hand. 'Yeah. Man's a cunt.'

'Yeah but why sniff around looking for landing places with us two on board?'

'How about because he's thick as pigshit?'

'A lot of blokes act thick round here, John. Doesn't mean to say they are. You know how you find a fucking idiot in the country?'

'How?'

'Take him with you.'

'Thanks a bunch. What else we find out?'

Vic decided to keep his mouth shut about Eype and Doochy. He took a swig of his pint of Branscombe. 'You know what, John?'

'What?'

'I thought you were getting better but now you're beginning to piss me off.'

'Oh yeah?' The round chin lifting. 'What about?'

'You and Scrump. Like two black dogs. Fight on sight.'

'So?'

'You can't go on like this, John –'

'Why not? Churchill did –'

'Fuck's Churchill got to do with it?'

'Him and De Gaulle. Hated each other, all through the fucking war –'

'Yeah but you're not Churchill –'

'And he's not fucking De Gaulle either –'

'You're supposed to be a copper, John. Not the fucking Terminator –'

Cromer smiled.

Joe came in looking relieved. 'He's taken it. Fifty quid a day for ten days –'

Cromer knocked back his pint and stood up. Grinning at Vic he put on a gruff accent: 'I'll be back –'

22

That evening Joe and Cath brought over a couple of two-pound lobsters. Cath showed Ellie how to kill them by stabbing them in the indented cross mark halfway down the head and they had them grilled with unsalted Normandy butter on the half-shell. Vic got out a couple of cold bottles of Jurançon Sec and they ate in the small kitchen at the back of the cottage.

Vic said, 'What d'you think Scrump's up to, Joe?'

'Oh my God,' said Ellie. 'Never marry a copper –'

'Bit late now,' said Cath.

'Hang on a minute –'

'The thing about Scrump is he always likes to look as if he's on to something – he's that sort of bloke, likes to look big, needs to be one up. He's probably in the King of Prussia now telling his mates how he wound up these two Bristol smartarses.'

'You think he knew we were coppers?'

'He wouldn't care if you were. Yeah, he's a bit of a villain and a chancer, but basically he doesn't give a toss, goes at things bullheaded, never thinks he's going to get pulled –'

Cath said, 'He was a good-looking man when he was younger –'

Joe said, 'Yeah, maybe that was his downfall. Everything came too easy – including the cider –'

Cath said, 'Oh come on, Joe, he's not all bad – he did us all those favours over the house –'

'Yeah but even there, Cath, he had to make it look he was doing it on the sly, cash in hand, all that – sort of bloke he is, he *likes* to look bent – typical loser, really –'

Vic said, 'So what's he want with the boat?'

Joe shrugged. 'Bit of poaching, picking up other buggers' pots, illegal sharkfishing charters – anything a bit dodgy –'

'He was talking about money. He into smuggling?'

Joe shook his head. 'Not your sort, Vic. They all grow their own grass round here –'

'As I found out –'

'Guys you're interested in got their own set-up if they got any sense. Nobody's going to take on a shambling fifty-year-old pisshead, are they?'

'Probably not.'

'Anyway,' said Joe, 'if Scrump goes anywhere interesting, I'll know.'

'How?'

Joe grinned. 'You know I showed him how to put the waypoints into the satnav?'

'So?'

'I didn't show him how to take them out, did I? Anywhere Scrump goes on satnav or auto pilot, any wreck or shore mark he picks, they'll all be recorded in the memory.'

Vic said, 'Suppose he doesn't?'

'What?'

'Use satnav.'

'We'll still have his compass and DRs.'

Ellie said, 'What's DR?'

'Dead reckoning,' said Joe. 'You multiply the boat speed by the heading and –'

'I knew it,' said Ellie. 'I should never have asked –'

Joe took out a Biro:

'No,' said Cath. 'No drawing on the tablecloth –'

Vic said, 'It's all right it's only paper –'

'Yes,' said Cath, 'and once he starts he never stops.'

'All right.' Joe put the Biro back in his pocket. 'All it means is, you have to know where you are so you know how to get back. You could have a sudden fret, you could have a breakdown, you could get stuck out at night – even Scrump knows that –'

Ellie, 'What's a fret?'

'A sea fog. Comes down suddenly. It'll be perfectly fine one minute, the next nothing, white-out. Doesn't happen inland –'

'Oh,' said Ellie. 'Anybody want coffee?'

Vic said, 'I'll do it.'

'Wonders never cease.'

Vic thought Ellie was looking flushed so he put a couple of extra measures in the cafetière. 'Calvados, anybody?'

'Yeah,' said Cath. 'Why not?'

'Let's go in the sitting room, leave all this –'

'Why?' said Ellie. 'Who's going to do it?'

'I am. Who else?'

In the sitting room, Ellie slipped her shoes off and tucked her legs up underneath her on the sofa. Cath sat beside her and Joe and Vic took the two old Ercol armchairs. Ellie said, 'Tell them about John and that bloke he thought was into S&M.'

'Why?'

'Oh come on love, just tell 'em –'

Vic thought Ellie was getting pissed and wondered about the baby. Cath read his thoughts: 'Doesn't do any harm once in a while –'

'What doesn't?'

'Never mind, love,' said Cath. 'Go on Vic.'

Vic told them about going to see Wally Allington in Bristol: '. . . And then I said, "So you're not into S&M then?" and he said, "For God's sake, Sergeant, what d'you think we are, per–"'

Ellie sat up with a start clutching on to Cath's arm – a roar of diesel noise – a scatter of gravel against the garden fence – Vic was up on his feet and out through the unlatched front door –

Fifty yards away a red and white RAV 4 was scrabbling up the shingle bank of the sea-defence wall, gravel spraying everywhere. Vic was out to the front gate as the RAV reached the compacted top of the bank and drove off left and out of sight towards East Cliff. Standing at the gate, breathing in the cold night air:

You're getting too fucking jumpy, Hallam –

Back inside, he snicked the latch on and down. Joe was standing facing him in the hall: 'You were off like a longdog there, mate –'

'Yeah, just some idiot in a four-wheel drive trying to beat the shingle –'

'Always get one or two – we had a Range Rover stuck in the tide last year, sea right up to the wheel arches, had to get the gravel-yard dragline to pull it out –'

'Stupid fucker –'

They went back into the sitting room. Ellie seemed unconcerned and was opening a packet of Dorchester Chocolate Gingers. 'Too much testosterone, if you ask me –'

Vic said, 'Who, me?'

'No, not you – bighead –'

'Who then?'

'John. Cromer.'

'Why?' Vic, still listening for the sound of tyres on gravel, didn't make the connection.

'Because of what's happened to him,' said Ellie. 'All that . . . that rage flying round, nowhere to go –'

Vic said, 'No need to play silly buggers is there? You saw him Joe. Couldn't stop needling old Scrump –'

'Scrump was enjoying himself, winding the kid up –'

Cath said, 'It's what men do. Look at our Ben. Eighteen. He tries it on all the time with Joe. Joe says one thing, Ben'll say the opposite, just to get him going – it's like stags and that, banging their heads together –'

Joe said, 'He knows when to stop though.'

Vic said. 'Yeah, but you find out bugger-all antagonising people –'

Ellie said, 'You're a sergeant, he's a sergeant. Simple as that. You should try working in a hospital, my lad. You get promoted, made up to Sister, you're poison –'

'Yeah but that's women, isn't it?'

Cath and Ellie looked at one another and shook their heads. Cath said, 'All men try to make themselves look bigger –'

Joe said, 'What about women?'

Ellie said, 'Women don't –'

'Bollocks,' said Vic.

Ellie looked at Cath. 'The ego has landed.'

Cath said, 'Ellie's right. Most women would sooner avoid any sort of a confrontation even if it means lying about it –'

Joe said, ' "I've got a headache." '

'When have I ever said that?'

'Well –'

The RAV 4 came roaring back. Down the shingle and past the house. Vic forced himself to sit still.

Ellie said, 'What's going on?'

Vic said, 'Some teenage pisshead in a RAV 4 – arsing about in the gravel –'

Ellie said, 'I had one of them up my backside all the

way from Dorchester. They see you're a woman they get on the dual carriageway, come right up alongside and bloody well sit there –'

'You see the driver?'

'Tinted windows, wasn't it?' She turned to Cath. 'What a wanker –'

'Probably –'.

'What colour was it?'

'Red with white stripes and a white soft-top.'

Vic heard himself say, 'This one was black.'

When they left, half an hour later, Vic and Joe walked down the path together while Ellie helped Cath on with her coat in the doorway. Joe saw Vic looking up at the gravel bank and down into the car park where Joe had parked his Land-Rover pick-up. 'What colour was it, Vic?'

'Red and white.'

Joe nodded. 'I'll ask around.'

'Thanks mate.'

23

Vic took the lobster remains out to the metal bin in the narrow back yard. The bin was under a corrugated plastic lean-to built out from the house to a breeze-block wall that held back most of the rain and mud running off the steep slope of East Cliff. There were no houses above them, only the rough hillocky grass and bramble of the cliff crowned by the old golf-club car park some three hundred feet above. Even so, Vic found himself looking up at the scatter of stars and listening to the teeth-sucking hiss and long-drawn-out snore of the sea withdrawing through the shingle – and realised he was waiting for some other noise, human noise – a slithering foot, a muffled grunt . . .

Nothing –

He went back into the kitchen, put the dishes and the grill pan in the sink to soak. Outside the intruder light went off; Vic switched off the kitchen light and stared into the blackness.

Too fucking jumpy by far –

The staircase was built in the gap between kitchen and sitting room: it was an old-fashioned arrangement,

and when the cottages were built it would probably
have been no more than a rough ladder to the loft and
thatch. Now it opened on to a narrow landing with
the main bedroom to the front and a small bedroom
and bathroom at the back. The old plaster and lath
ceilings had been removed and both rooms slanted up
to the scarred, black-painted ridge beam. Lying in
bed looking at the ceiling was like being a kid again,
sleeping in a high white tent –

Ellie was asleep naked under a single sheet, her
body spread opulent and negligent across most of the
bed, her lips slightly parted. It was a fond, secretive
smile, as if she were reliving pleasant childish
memories. Vic never tired of watching her. Sometimes she awoke under the tension of his gaze, but
when Vic asked her what she had been dreaming
about, the answer was always a mumbled 'Nothing'
or 'Can't remember', and she would fall instantly
asleep again, mouth curved and vague as the Mona
Lisa.

Vic slid in beside her, watched her for a few
seconds, then quietly switched off the bedside lamp.
He moved against her hot body and lay there safe and
thankful. She stirred, turned to face him, her breasts
burning hot against him, and without opening her
eyes, pulled him on top of her and fumbled him inside
her. Not for the first time, Vic felt himself both moved
and estranged by the depth and simplicity of her
sexual nature: she moved like the sea, and he was the
proverbial idiot-shackled-to-a-monster struggling to

stay afloat – and then, as he came, drowning out of sheer fucking gratitude –

How could you love someone and never know what they really felt? Maybe you just had to live with them and then bit by bit you'd find out – if you were lucky –

Vic eased himself off her, but instead of falling mindlessly asleep as he had expected, he lay wide away – and fearful.

When Ellie began to breathe through her mouth, he slid out of bed, lifted his dressing gown off the hook on the door and padded downstairs for a glass of Perrier.

Instead he found himself smoking three or four Marlboro one after another and finishing the bottle of Calvados. He lay shivering on the sofa, naked under his dressing gown, besieged by waking nightmares and wondering in between the self-induced scenarios of car crashes, rape, accidental abortion and bodies on slabs, whether it was the Calvados or the lobster or the coffee – or that fucking RAV 4 –

You've got so much, Hallam – and all it means is you've got so much more to fucking lose –

Finally, at half past three, he dragged himself back to bed.

'Vic!'

'Whassat?'

'Wake up! Sam's on the bloody phone, I'm late for bloody work and you said you'd do the washing-up!'

He stumbled stiff-legged and bleary down the stairs to hear Ellie slam the door.

'Sam?'

The hiss of a car phone: 'Morning Vic. All well?'

Vic tried to clear the roughness from his throat. 'Yeah –'

'Sounds like it – having a little lie-in, were we –'

Fuck off Sam –

'Forgot to do the washing-up, did we –'

Fuck off and die –

'Yeah yeah yeah. Very funny –'

'Well here's something else you can laugh at. It's all coming on top tonight –'

'What?'

'Tonight or tomorrow night – there's no fucking moon apparently – get Cromer, get your arse in gear and call me at the fucking office –'

'Right –'

'And Vic –'

'What?'

'Leave the washing-up till later.'

24

First thing Vic saw was the red and white RAV 4 at the foot of East Beach car park. As he snicked the garden gate shut a burly red-haired figure backed out of the driver's seat and gestured him to hurry up –

Chant. Steven Chant – the night nurse off the *Aware* –

'What the fuck –?'

Chant pulled off a latex glove and stuck out his hand. 'DC Shand, seconded to the Met –'

'Fuck my old boots –'

'I know – I was told to keep schtum –'

'You got a first name?'

'Steve –'

Vic glanced at the RAV 4: it had to be the same vehicle as last night but now the big white bull-bars had been shoved right back into the radiator. 'Where d'you get this bloody thing?'

'Off the bastards hijacked one of our prison vans, top of Eggardon. I was in the follow car, driver's still up there on Scene of Crime. I was told to contact you and DS Cromer. Van was shot to fuck but this was drivable so I brought it down here –'

'This was one of their vehicles?'

'Yeah, one of three. Where's DS Cromer?'

'I'll direct you –' Vic reached for the passenger handle. Shand's big freckled paw closed round Vic's wrist. 'Sorry.' Shand put the latex glove back on. 'After this I'm taking it to Forensic – Operation Shit-Fan has just occurred –'

'Right. Follow the white Cavalier –'

Cromer was outside his mobile home in a black Megadeth tour shirt and tan boxers pouring a carton of milk down his throat.

'For fuck's sake, John – I'm feeling sick enough already –'

'Fuck's going on?'

'Don't ask –'

'Sam's tearing his hair out –'

'John – DC Steve Shand –' Vic left them to it, piled into the mobile home, grabbed the phone and punched the intercom speaker button. 'Sam – Vic –'

'The fuck kept you – been doing the fucking hoovering?'

'Met up with DC Shand –'

'The Met guy?'

'Yeah –'

Thanks for telling me –

'He there?'

'Coming –'

'Put him on –'

Vic held out the phone. 'All yours, Steve.' Vic

glanced at Cromer. 'Got any coffee on? I feel like home-made shit –'

Between Sam's barked metallic questions and DC Shand's clipped 'Yes-sir-no-sir' replies, Vic managed to get the gist of it. Shand was right: 'Operation Shit-Fan' was one cock-up after another –

It had started, apparently, with a tip-off from what Sam called 'some fucking anonymosity from MI5' that a big drop was imminent. This was 'driven', according to Steve Shand, by what he termed 'movements' in Belgrade and somewhere called Chişinău which was the capital of Moldova. Sam said this was fucking news to him and how the fuck did DC Shand know all this? Shand said he had been with the MPs in Kosovo. Sam said since when did we have fucking MPs in Kosovo? Shand explained that he had been a redcap with Military Intelligence before joining the Force and had then been seconded to the Met side of Operation Kingfisher because he was fluent in Serbo-Croat. Unfortunately, he said, Albanians spoke Albanian.

Sam said, 'That's the first then.'

Shand said, 'What's that, sir?'

'Cock-up. Where the fuck you learn Serbo-Croat anyway – and don't tell me Oxford because if there's one thing I can't stand it's graduate fucking coppers –'

'No sir. Belgrade. I was born there, left when I was eight. My father was an economics lecturer. He didn't agree with Milosevic so Milosevic had him killed by the JSO in ninety-one.'

'Fuck's the JSO?'

'Special Operations – they call themselves the Red Berets –'

'Fucking cheek –'

'They're a death and snatch squad, sir. Supposed to be police but they're nearly all crims. They shot the last Prime Minister Djindjic and ran the drugs trade with the Zemun clan –'

'Zemun?'

'The ones we're after, sir. The guy who killed Duchene was in with them. And the ones who beat him up –'

'How do you know, DC Shand?'

'The Met had me bug the sickbay and their cells, sir.'

'But you don't speak Albanian?'

'The Met know some people who do, sir.'

'So why the fuck didn't they tell me?'

'Reasons of security, sir –'

'Cock-up number fucking two.'

'I couldn't say, sir. I only got the information after this morning's operations, sir –'

'You couldn't say, Shand, but I fucking can – because of this tip-off on the drop I was told to get these Balkanians out the Verne and into our high-security cells in Horfield, Bristol.'

'Yes sir.'

'So I'm the one carrying the fucking can –'

'Sir?'

'I said I'm the one carrying the fucking can for the

fact that you and your fucking . . . colleagues, DC Shand . . . let these four fucking Balkanian homicidal maniacs loose this morning –'

'With respect, sir, we didn't let them loose – it was a classic three-car guerilla ambush –'

Sam bellowing over the intercom: '*I don't give a fuck whether it was a fucking ambush or a fucking gorillas' tea party – it's major cock-up number three –*'

Vic and Cromer could hear Sam breathing himself down . . .

'Tell me, DC Shand – are you Yugoslavian, Serbian or what?'

'British, sir.'

'*British?*'

'Yes sir. After my father's death my mother and I came over as asylum seekers.'

Sam fell silent.

Cromer's kettle boiled and whistled.

Sam cleared his throat. 'D'you mind if I ask you something?'

'No sir.'

'Why did you join up, son?'

'Sir?'

'What I mean is, was it because of your father?'

'Yes sir. Partly sir.'

'I'm going to apologise to you, DC Shand –'

'Yes sir, thank you sir –'

'But don't think that means I didn't mean what I just said about cock-ups.'

'No sir.'

'Take us through the events of this morning if you will.' A momentary cessation of signal as a recorder was plugged in and then Sam's voice, sounding closer, warmer, less metallic: 'In your own time, son —'

DC Shand said that because the previous day had been his leave day the procedure was that his opposite number, Allie Sullivan, did a double shift. Since there was no one in sickbay and only the four Albanians in solitary, Allie had had a quiet night and volunteered for the four hours' escort duty to Bristol and back. Sam said Allie sounded a bugger for punishment if he'd already done a double shift and was volunteering for more. Shand said because Allie had done the two shifts he would be getting paid triple time. He said Allie told him getting eighty quid overtime for sitting in a van for four hours was 'a piece a piss'. Sam said was that relevant, and Shand said sometimes Allie needed the money and sometimes he couldn't be arsed. Vic said that apart from the financial obligations Sam knew about, Allie had a heavy betting habit and Shand said not any more he didn't.

Sam told Shand to get on with it.

Shand said Allie had opted to travel in the back of the van with the prisoners and an armed prison officer. There were two more armed prison officers in the cab, one driving. Shand and another prison officer, both unarmed, were in the prison officer's own Toyota Corolla travelling behind. Shand said he had the emergency paramedic kit with him in case of accidents.

The prison van was a regulation unmarked white Mercedes Vito with strengthened side doors and tailgate, no windows but two grilled ventilators in the roof. The prisoners were link-chained as for hospital and court appearances and sat on benches each side. Allie and the prisoner officer sat with their backs to the cab facing them. A regulation Elsan-type toilet was bolted to the floor at the rear with its own plastic slider and automatic Ventaxia fan circulation.

Sam said that was new and Shand said it was EU rules for the transportation of prisoners. Sam said what a fucking country.

Shand said as per regulations for the avoidance of built-up areas where an extra police escort would be required, they cut through behind Weymouth on to the Dorchester bypass and then forked left just before Winterbourne Abbas on to the old single track that would lead them, eventually, past Yeovil on to the A37 for Bristol. Shand said this was normal practice for the route –

'You mean anybody could know about it?'

'Yes sir.'

'And did they?'

'Yes sir. Obviously sir.'

'Thank you, Shand. Cock-up number four –'

'Yes sir.'

'Go on –'

Shand said as they got to the right turn to Compton Valence a Land-Rover pulled out between the van and the Toyota. Sam said that was pretty dozy fucking driving on the part of the prison officer and Shand said not necessarily sir, since the Land-Rover continued to signal a right turn and he and the prison officer assumed the Land-Rover was a local farm vehicle taking an immediate right on to the West Compton-Wynford Eagle turn-off.

Sam said, 'Cock-up number five.'

Shand said, 'The turn-off was only fifty yards ahead –'

Sam said, 'Never assume nothing.'

Shand said that as the Mercedes van came up to the turn-off, a black Range Rover pulled out in front of it and then the RAV 4, following up fast behind the Range Rover, T-boned the Mercedes van into the left-hand hedge. At the same time the Land-Rover in front of the Corolla braked hard and two dark-haired men jumped out and legged it for the Mercedes van –

'And what did you do?'

'We braked hard as well sir, and then reversed as fast as we could –'

'Why?'

'Prison officer's own car sir. Practically brand new.'

'Jesus Christ –'

'With respect sir, neither of us was armed –'

'Were the two men?'

'I didn't see then but I had reason to believe so later.'

'Did you?'

'Yes sir. It was a classic three vehicle set-up sir – one to block, one to hit, one to get away –'

'It was a classic cock-up, DC Shand. Number six if I'm not mistaken.'

'Yes sir. If you say so sir –'

'Continue.'

'Well sir, after we stopped, I got the paramedic bag and ran towards the Land-Rover in front of us –'

'And your . . . colleague?'

'In the car on his mobile for immediate assistance, sir.'

'But miles from anywhere?'

'Yes sir.'

'Then what?'

'There were a few pops and bangs sir.'

' "Pops and bangs"?'

'Yes sir. Pops like silenced pistols, bangs like doors being slammed or kicked.'

'So what did you do?'

'Ducked sir. Behind the rear Land-Rover, sir.'

'Very wise . . . And?'

'When I heard the black Range Rover start to drive off, sir, I went forward. I saw the sliding door in the body of the van had been shot out and forced open –'

'From inside or out?'

'Both sir. Also it had been wrecked by the impact sir. With the RAV 4. I didn't see much of the impact because of the rear Land-Rover but that's my opinion –'

'My opinion: all part of the same on-going cock-up –'

'Yes sir. I looked in the van and . . .' Shand stopped. Vic and Cromer heard him swallow.

'Take your time, son.'

'By the smell sir, Allie Sullivan and the armed prison officer with him had been blinded with pepper spray. No sign of the prisoners, but the officer's belt had been severed, and his sidearm, holster and keys had been removed. As a result he was bleeding from a gash across the stomach. As I was attending to him I saw the communicating wire-glass grille between the cab and the back of the van had been smashed and the armed officers in front had also been sprayed and slashed –'

'Hang on a minute. From inside or out?'

'Inside, sir. The two officers had been slashed on the back of the neck and side of the face –'

'Knives?'

'Lunes, sir.'

' "Lunes"?'

'Yes sir. They're a weapon, sir.'

'Never heard of 'em.'

'Well sir, basically the classic Albanian lune is a half-moon of Chinese surgical steel bolted to a brass knuckleduster –'

'I know you're going to tell me, Shand, but why Chinese?'

'Only country that would trade with Albania, sir.'

Cromer nudged Vic: 'All comes back to fucking politics –'

Sam said, 'Who said that?'

Vic said, 'Nobody –'

Cromer said, 'Politicians and their poxy money-grabbing fucking wars and we're the fucking punch-bag in the middle –'

'That you Cromer?'

'Yes sir.'

'Shut the fuck up. Shand, where they get these things?'

'They make them sir. In the prison workshops –'

'Fucking great –'

'Albanians have had to be their own gunsmiths for years, sir – they're dab hands with the metalworking tools –'

Sam grunted, then: 'They make fucking pepper-spray cans as well do they?'

'No sir. Standard Verne issue.'

'Where the fuck –'

'I'm coming to that sir.'

'Please do.'

'Well sir, after I applied emergency dressings I saw the prison officer in the back wasn't all that badly wounded –'

'Only slashed across the gut –'

'I went to the cab of the van. By now the black Range Rover had gone. As I said, sir, the two officers there had also been sprayed and slashed – as I attended to them they confirmed it was by the prisoners in the back of the van –'

'What the other two Balkanian fuckpigs doing then?'

'Shooting out the tyres of the rear Land-Rover and van while the prisoners forced their way out of the buckled side-door –'

'And you saw nothing?'

'Van was at an angle, sir. They were gone when I got there.'

'Lunes, pepper spray, fucking *guns* – and not a single prison officer managed to do anything about it – what a fucking Godalmighty cock-up, Shand –'

'With respect sir, it was all over in seconds, and in any case that's not quite true sir.'

'How is it "not quite true"?'

'Allie Sullivan –'

'Your mucker?'

'. . . Yes sir. He had two more sprays in his jacket pocket.'

'Let me get this straight. You're saying –'

'Not just me, sir. General belief now is Sullivan was in on the whole thing from leaving the shower door open for Duchene to get done over, letting his killer into sickbay to top him, then facilitating the prisoners' escape –'

' "General belief"?'

'Yes sir – according to the Met analysis of the tape transcripts –'

Sam said, 'Stop there a minute. I hope you're listening to this, Hallam –'

'Yes Sam.'

'As I recall, this Allie is the same bloke you "persuaded" to cosy up to these fucking Balkanians?'

'Yes Sam.'

'Looks like you persuaded him only too fucking well –'

'Yes Sam.'

'The little fucker conned you, didn't he? He never had intention of repaying any fucking money, did he? He conned you left right and centre –'

'Yes Sam.'

'One fuck-up after another, isn't it?'

'Yes Sam.'

'Make me feel better, Hallam – tell me you fucked up –'

'I fucked up, Sam.'

'Thank you. Put Shand back on will you?'

'Yes Sam.'

'Now then Shand, when you put this "general belief" to this Allie character –'

'I couldn't sir –'

'What the fuck –'

'That was the reason I requested information from the Met transcripts, sir –'

'What fucking reason you talking about, Shand?'

'His throat was cut. He was dead sir.'

25

Shand peered at the intercom. 'What's that clicking noise?'

Vic said, 'Sam's tapping his teeth with a ballpoint pen.'

Cromer said, 'He does that when he's thinking.'

Sam's voice: 'After all Allie does for them, they cut his throat. Any idea why, Shand?'

'He was surplus to requirements, sir.'

'There's gratitude –'

'The Zemun are a criminal clan, sir. They're not a gang, they're more like a family, only stronger. You don't belong, you're disposable.'

Sam said, 'I suppose you think them slitting his gizzard lets you off the hook, Hallam –'

'No Sam, I don't –'

'Good – because apart from anything else, we've now got another fucking murder inquiry on our hands. Who's dealing with it, Shand?'

'Local CID sir.'

'Not Poole or Winfrith?'

'Not at this stage, sir.'

'Right. Now I want you all listening to this because in five minutes' time I shall be rushing round like a

186

blue-arsed fly. According to our nameless MI5 friend this drop's coming on top tonight or tomorrow. They've tracked this wagon across Europe and it's arriving in Poole Freight Park with a container full of heroin. Poole Freight Park's on our patch so I'm coordinating –'

Vic said, 'Sam –'

'That you, Hallam?'

'Yes Sam.'

'You realise I'm in the middle of giving you a briefing?'

'I know, Sam –'

'An *urgent* fucking briefing –'

'I know, Sam, but –'

'This had better not be another of your fucking cock-ups –'

Cromer and Shand were looking at him: Shand surprised, Cromer frowning – both getting ready to distance themselves . . .

Cock-up or no cock-up, you don't speak now Hallam, you've let yourself and Doochy down –

'If you've got something to say, Hallam, get on and fucking say it will you? I haven't got all fucking *day* –'

'I think there could be a drop coming off at Eype –'

'You don't sound too sure, Hallam. Where the fuck's Eype?'

'Mile up the coast –'

'How'd you get this fucking mad idea?'

'What Doochy said. His last words. I told you –'

'You told me he said something about a fucking pipe –'

'He said "A pipe" –'

'Fucking hell, Hallam –'

'I think he meant "Up Eype" – I think that was what he was trying to tell me –'

'*You think?* Holy shit –'

Vic looked at Cromer. 'A lot of people get the pronunciation wrong, Sam.'

Vic waited. Reluctantly, Cromer leaned forward and said, 'I thought it was "Ipe", Sam –'

'Oh Christ, Cromer, not you as fucking well –'

Cromer said nothing.

Sam said, 'Vic – can you get a container wagon in there?'

'No, it's a gravel beach –'

'There you are then – end of story –'

'I don't think that's what Doochy had in mind. He told me the whole idea was to get in and out fast –'

'Fucking hell Vic –'

'Look Sam, I wouldn't have mentioned it if I didn't think –'

'All right Vic, I give in. How d'you spell this Eype place?'

'E-Y-P-E.'

'Right. I've made a note and I'll mention it. Now fuck off and let me brief these guys in peace will you?'

*

Vic stood outside the mobile home looking at the RAV 4. After a minute Shand came out pulling on his latex gloves. 'Cromer's typing up the bumf.'

'Yeah.'

'For what it's worth, I think you were right –'

'What about?'

'Sticking up for yourself.' Shand grinned. 'Not sure whether I would –'

'Yeah, well you don't know Sam like I do.' Vic watched Shand straighten the plastic seat and floor covers. 'How d'you get on with Allie, Steve?'

'I didn't. I was told the drill on this job was eyes open, gob shut. Allie needed the chat to figure the angles –'

'Yeah. Ever-helpful Allie. Poor bastard –'

'All I can say to that is he was the one left the sickbay door open.'

'You know that for sure do you?'

'He finished his shift, went on his grass run. In and out of solitary. One of 'em gives him the message, he comes back, gets his keys, opens Doochy's door, puts his keys back in the lock-up . . . He had everything figured but you coming back early. Met's got it on the transcripts –'

'You tape all that stuff with me and Doochy?'

'Had to. You did a good job there –'

'Not good enough as it turned out.'

'I got to tell you something Vic. They were never going to let Doochy go.'

'Who weren't?'

'Neither us nor them.'

'What d'you mean?'

'We were holding back an extradition order.'

'Where from?'

'The States.'

Fucking suckered again, Hallam − all that fucking time wasted − all that shit about getting Doochy home . . . You bastard, Sam . . . No, it wasn't Sam, it was the whole fucking mob, the whole fucking deal . . . Anybody's a cunt, Hallam, you are −

'What about this skinny guy did Doochy, tried to do me?'

'Ramiz was the one who had Doochy beaten up −'

'Because they wanted in on this smack-for-crack deal −'

'They didn't just want in, Vic, they wanted all of it. Doochy wouldn't play because he knew his mates would kill him.'

'Nice mates. Do we know who they are?'

'Met are looking at the North London Yardies and a bunch of ex-Russian *Mafiya* from Moldova and the Ukraine. They're all over West London. They got the money, Yardies got the muscle. The Zemun are in with the Albanians running the big-money vice rackets up and down the UK. They're the competition, the new guys on the block. Each mob's trying to off the other to control the whole UK heroin and coke supply. They corner the market and trouser the proceeds. Winner takes all. What makes it worse for us is the Zemun's a lot hungrier −'

'Why's that?'

'They're the ones who knocked off President Djindjic.'

'So?'

'They shit and fell back in it –'

'How come?'

'Djindjic was a president who was big on reform. He wanted the rats out of the granary. Zemun wanted a new Milosevic so they assassinated him. But it turned out Djindjic had more support than they thought. The result was a big crackdown on Zemun's H and coke network. You arrest the dealers you got no supply. Prices double and treble. Sixty quid a gram here, two hundred quid in sunny Serbia. Nice little killing for somebody –'

'Doochy being one of 'em –'

'Ramiz and his guys gave Doochy his chance but he blew it –'

'How? They were the ones hammering fuck out of him –'

'Way they saw it, that was his chance to join up.'

'Fuckin' hell –'

'They're not like us, Vic. The fact Doochy was black didn't help either. If those two guys had got to you in hospital you'd have been on the slab as well.'

'You think?'

Shand shook his head. 'I know. It's on the tapes. You were mentioned by name – Thomp-son.'

Fuck it – no point in thinking about it –

Vic made himself look at the caved-in white bull-bar and the channel-section bumper underneath. 'Could you do me a favour, Steve?'

'Such as?'

'Just feel around inside that bottom section there.'

Shand knelt and hooked his fingers under the bumper.

'Anything there?'

'Something –'

'Let's have a look –'

Shand drew out his clenched latex fist. Inside was a handful of pea gravel.

Vic said, 'I thought so –'

'What?'

'I clocked a red and white RAV 4 outside the cottage last night. Went straight up the shingle bank, came back later –'

'You reckon it's this one?'

'Not many around with a chassis full of shingle are there?'

Shand fished out an evidence bag and poured in the pea gravel. 'Could be they've been having a look at you –'

'Wouldn't be the first time. Last night Ellie – my missis – said a red and white RAV 4 followed her home.'

'I'll check it out, Vic –'

'Tyre marks are still there, all over the shingle bank.'

Shand pocketed the bag. 'What's your security like?'

'Lights – door-chains – window-locks –'

'No direct station link?'

'No point. Call goes through to Weymouth, they try to find the nearest patrol car within twenty miles. Most week-nights there's only three or four on –'

Shand nodded and bent down to the RAV 4's offside front tyre. With a gloved finger he picked away at the zig-zag tread. Underneath the earth and grass from the country lanes was a bedded-in layer of beach gravel. He stood up. 'According to the transcripts, when you knocked off their top man Ramiz –'

'The skinny guy?'

'When you did that, the rest of 'em didn't go a lot on it –'

'I can imagine.'

'I told you – they're not like us. They're a clan, a family. They like to know where people live –'

Vic felt the black wave pass over him.

Remembering Ellie in bed asleep, her naked arm flung out –

They like to know where people live –

26

Joe was on the quay by the knuckle. He had the bonnet up on Scrump's rust-streaked white Range Rover and was taking the rotor-arm off the distributor. He tossed it up in the air, caught it, dropped it in his shirt pocket. 'That'll stop the bastard.'

'What's happened, Joe? Where is he?'

'God knows. He took the boat out last night, last trace on the Harbour Office radar shows him doing ten knots due south.'

'Fuckin' hell.'

'Exactly.'

'Any ideas?'

'All depends how pissed up he was.' Joe took the strut down and let the alloy bonnet slam shut. 'If he's put a destination in the satnav we'll know where he's been when he comes back.'

'Fat lot of good that is.'

'Telling me.'

'Where's due south going to take him?'

'Well, if he stays awake, gets through both separation lanes, remembers to refuel and gets the tides right, he'll be somewhere west of Cherbourg.'

'If he doesn't?'

'He's going to pile up on Guernsey or end up in the Alderney Race with no fucking engine.'

'What's Cherbourg from here?'

'One sixty-five, one seventy –'

'East of south –'

'If you put in Portland as a waypoint.'

'Sounds like Cherbourg to me – all those booze warehouses –'

'Yeah . . .'

'You could always call the Douaniers –'

'Oh yeah, get the whole fucking boat confiscated –'

'You think that's his game?'

'Oh yeah – he's done it before, on the ferry. The white-van booze and fags run. Got done by Customs on that so now he's trying the fucking boat. I should've fucking *known* . . . Scrump all over – so fucking dumb he thinks he's clever . . .' Joe brought a fist down on the bonnet, looked at the dent he'd left. 'Oh fuck it. Fuck it, fuck it, fuck it –'

'Joe –'

'Sorry mate –'

'You could well be –'

'All because of fucking *money* . . . What did you say?'

'Never mind –'

'No, come on –'

'I was going to ask you to do something for me.'

'Such as?'

'You know that RAV 4 last night?'

'That the same one was there this morning, big ginger bloke sitting in it?'

'Yeah –'

Joe grinned. 'Copper written all over him.'

'Yeah . . . Look Joe, I can't say a lot more but we've got Game On for tonight. Probably all night. Can Ellie stay with you?'

'Course – Christ sake, Vic, why all the fucking palaver?'

'Those guys in the RAV 4. They were clocking our house. This morning they T-boned a paddywagon, slit a bloke's throat –'

'No shit?'

'They're hard cases, Joe. Serious hard cases. On the other hand, we're supposed to be taking their hairy arses out tonight . . . All the same –'

'Yeah, better safe than sorry.'

'Thanks Joe.'

'No problem mate.'

'I'll give Ellie a ring. If she asks you –'

'What?'

'Say I've got to be on obbo all night.'

They took Cromer's new Ford Focus RS. It was dark blue, had wide wheelarches and in the shifting sun-light some of the panels shone purple. Inside there was an alloy gear knob and pedals; the steering wheel and sports seats had inserts of bright blue leather. Following the heavy traffic on the road out of the harbour, the RS's suspension thudded over every rut and lump.

'Where d'you get this, John?'

Without looking at him Cromer said, 'You might have fucking mentioned it.'

'What?'

'Eype. Sam practically chewed my ear off. Said we were supposed to be working together. At least I fucking backed you up –'

'When?'

'On that "Ipe" thing.'

'Only when you had to, John.'

'*Because you didn't fucking tell me –*' Cromer's neck was going red.

Vic said, 'As I recall you were pissing me off –'

'What about?'

'Scrump in particular, your whole fucking attitude in general. Mardy-arsing round the fucking boat all afternoon. You don't get anything out of people by antagonising them, John.'

Cromer drove in silence.

Vic said, 'On the other hand, you're right. I should have told you. If that makes me a cunt, I'm a cunt . . . All over now, Baby Blue?'

'Yeah.' Cromer frowned. 'You're not the easiest bloke to get on with you know.'

'Never said I was. What did Sam think anyway?'

Cromer said, 'He doesn't go a lot on your Eype idea.'

'I didn't think he would. In his position I'm not sure I would. Fact remains they were Doochy's last words, and they either mean nothing or something. Who knows?'

Cromer went quiet. Then he said, 'I still see her face, you know. In Palmer Street when she was lying in my arms. She didn't say anything. No last words. She just looked at me, helpless.'

Vic thought, *You poor bastard – but you still went out and shot the fuckers didn't you?*

What he said was, 'Anyway, it's up to Sam now.'

'Yeah.'

At the roundabout they turned off towards Dorchester, Cromer not saying much, just humming to himself and fiddling with the seat adjustment.

Because there were clearly bridges still to mend and normal service to be resumed, Vic said, 'Where d'you get this thing anyway? Rides like a fucking brick –'

'Doesn't like going slow. It's on assessment, Motor Pool brought it down.'

'Bit fucking Essex for round here, my son.'

'All RSs are like this. It's called Imperial Blue.'

'Because it turns purple when the sun shines?'

'Because it's any colour you like so long as it's blue –'

'Doesn't say RS on the back –'

'Motor Pool took it off, said it was too boy-racer.'

'Any good?'

There was a gap in the traffic: Cromer smirked to himself and put his foot down. The RS took off and immediately the ride smoothed out.

'Holy shit –'

Cromer was saying it had over 200hp and did 0–60 faster than a Jag XK. Vic looked at him. He had a big silly grin on his face and they were doing ninety uphill on the A35.

Maybe he was still a kid after all –

'Next left to Eggardon, John.'

'I thought we were going to Winfrith HQ –'

'This is the pretty way. And I want to look at the crash site.'

'You don't trust any fucker do you?'

'What did Sam say to DC Shand?'

Cromer thought for a moment. ' "Never assume nothing." '

'That's right.'

Eggardon Hill was an amphitheatre, carved by nature out of chalk and too steep for anything but sheep. Driving towards the massive green ramparts of the old hill fort and looking down on the crows and occasional buzzards circling the sheep in the valley seven hundred feet below, Vic had the feeling that nothing had changed, not even the harsh grass lining the lynchets, for the last two thousand years. He told Cromer to stop at the crossroads and got out into the stiff breeze. To the south, the sea; to the north, beyond the forty-five degree slope, Powerstock Forest: old Dorset, rough and unyielding . . .

Cromer got out. 'Enjoying the view, are we?'

Vic said, 'Four tracks, north, east, south and west. Every one dipping out of sight within two hundred yards. Up there –' Vic pointed east towards the crash site; 'three more, ditto.'

'Handy for a getaway –'

'They recce'd it, John . . . Let's go and see what's left.'

All the vehicles had been removed. There were ruts in the grass; mud, rust, tyre fragments and crystals of broken glass had been swept into the verges. While Vic peered into the smashed hedge, Cromer searched the grass strip in the middle of the narrow track. He took out an evidence bag and used it to pick up a small metal cylinder. 'Here's one they missed.'

'What is it?'

Cromer looked at the ridged end. 'Nine mil.'

'Look at this, John –'

In amongst the crushed cow-parsley and the dark blue paint-scrapes on the buckled stone wall was a run of what looked like fresh creosote.

Cromer said, 'Hydraulic fluid?'

Vic took out a tissue and dabbed it at the wall. He sniffed it and held it out to Cromer.

'Blood?'

'Yeah,' said Vic. 'Probably Allie's.'

'How?'

'You get your throat cut you're going to lose a pint or two . . . RAV 4 hits the van, van hits the wall, tips – out it comes.'

'Oh shit.'

'Yeah. Now for the hard part –'

'What? Forensic have done it all –'

'They won't have told Allie's mother.' Vic tossed the stained tissue back in the hedge. 'They never do.'

When they parked outside the terraced house down the road from Bushells Wines they saw a milk bottle still on the red Cardinal-polished doorstep. Vic rang the bell. No reply.

Vic said, 'Go round the back, John. See if there's a window you can open.'

He lit a Marlboro, looked at his watch. Half ten. No one about.

Waiting, smoking: remembering all the other doorsteps he'd stood on –

A rattle of the chain and the door swung open. Cromer's face was pale but hard-set. He stepped aside to show Vic the frail, aproned figure crumpled at the foot of the stairs. She still had one slipper on. The other lay in the tiled hall in a long pool that ran from the stairs to the table with the china figure of Jesus, his hand raised in benediction.

'She's had her throat cut, Vic.'

27

Vic kept his eye on the speedo. They were barrelling along at seventy through the wooded back lanes to Winfrith. Cromer braked late into the upcoming S-bend. The RS went through the bends on rails. Frowning to himself and shaking his head, he kept the speed down to fifty.

'Something wrong, John?'

'Why do an old lady? I can't get my head round it –'

'That's how they are. They wouldn't think twice about it.'

They're not like us. They like to know where people live –

'Fucking savages, Vic . . . Doochy, that girl with her gut cut open, Allie, his poor old ma. All for fucking *money*.' The road straightened and ran through a dark conifer plantation, the asphalt still black with damp. Cromer rammed the RS up through the gears. 'I'd like to savage a few of the bastards – specially the ones did that old lady –'

'Christ sake John, don't go fucking AWOL on me now –'

'That supposed to fucking mean?'

'What it means, John, is that you still haven't got Opal out of your system . . . in my opinion.'

Silence.

Then Cromer said, 'In your opinion?'

'Yes.'

'Well, fuck your opinion.'

Their speed crept up over seventy. A T-junction sign was hidden in the unclipped trees. Cromer slammed his foot on the brake. The tyres screeched along the wet road. By the time they stopped they were halfway across the junction and Cromer's face was red down to his shirt collar.

Vic said, 'Nearly right.'

Cromer said, 'Sorry about that. Missed the fucking sign –'

'I had noticed.'

Cromer grinned. 'You old bastard.'

Vic looked back at the forty yards of dried tarmac and black rubber they'd left on the road behind them: 'Anyway, just to get back to this Eype thing – so you can't say I never tell you anything –'

'Fucking hell, you don't give up, do you?'

'Doochy told me they'd knocked his cut down from five per cent to half a per cent. He thought it was a right fucking liberty, because it still included organising the drop. So he was calling the shots on this one. "You want it, you come and get it." That's why these fuckers beat him up –'

'To knock it out of him?'

Vic nodded. 'I reckon he'd already picked his spot. Eype.'

Cromer thought it over. 'I can't see them going for it.'

'Somebody's got to – even if it's only us.'

'From what Sam said they're all fixated on this fucking Freight Park.'

The briefing room was away from the main HQ in a two-storey brick building on the site of the old Winfrith Nuclear Research Establishment: there were black and yellow barriers and speed bumps on every access road.

Inside, all the blinds had been pulled down and thirty grey plastic chairs had been set out in a semi-circle around two overhead projectors and four swivelling whiteboards. Three-quarters of the chairs were occupied by a mixture of Drug and Vice Squad men and women in plainclothes and Marine Police in uniform. The front row remained empty. Sam Richardson sat behind a trestle table on a dais with a couple of plainclothes high-ups from the Met and a uniformed Chief Super. Vic noticed they all had black leather swivel office chairs; a fifth swivel chair with a telescopic alloy pointer on it remained empty between the twin screens.

Vic and Cromer took middle seats at the back with a good view of the projector screens. A tall athletic-looking man in a black overall with a Glock automatic holstered in his belt-rig strode on to the dais, smiled –

very white, beautifully even teeth – at his superiors and took the fifth swivel chair.

Vic nudged Cromer. 'Him again.'

'Cunt who fucked us up the arse in Palmer Street.'

'Steve Humphries.'

'Yeah –'

Eight more SFOs – Specialised Firearms Officers – filed in and took the front row of grey plastic chairs. They too were wearing black overalls. Unlike Humphries they were unarmed and carrying armfuls of heavy black metal-cased portable radios –

Same as the ones screaming out 'Bandits!' in Palmer Street –

What had happened then was that Steve Humphries, positioned opposite in number 25, had delayed the order to fire until the target van, full of armed Turks, had rolled to a stop. The idea was, he said, to catch them hands-on. It left Vic and Cromer exposed in number 14. In the few seconds before the shit started to fly, two other Turks stationed in the back yard of number 14 had seen Opal moving from the back room to the front. They shot her in the back, twice: she died in Cromer's arms.

Now Steve Humphries was grinning his white teeth at them.

Sam Richardson stood up. 'Right. That's it. Welcome all. Now listen up. What we're looking at here is a one-night operation, possibly two –'

A low, surprised mutter; Sam held up both palms for quiet. 'I know, I know – we all want to be back with our nearest and dearest, but the simple fact of the matter is: we can't. The reason for that is, as I'm sure you'll all appreciate, we can't trust these foreign gentlemen to turn up on time. It could be tonight, it could be tomorrow night – both nights, as you will be aware by now, are moonless. However, as you will not be aware for very good security reasons, everybody in this room will be CB until end-ops. For those of you younger than me this means confined to barracks, that is here, in these glorious surroundings, until end of operations. Bunk beds in separate dormitories are being provided upstairs.' Sam glanced at Steve Humphries. 'Detective Inspector Humphries' SFOs –'

Vic said, 'Fucker's been promoted –'

Cromer said, 'Cunt.'

Sam said, '– will now pass amongst you issuing your portable radios. These have automatic frequency shift to avoid detection by in-vehicle scanners. They are linked to main COMMS which is encrypted for similar reasons. Mobiles will not, repeat not, be used, and I must ask you, if they are not switched off already, to switch them off now.'

Another murmur. Sam raised his voice over it: 'Your stations will be told should operations continue the full forty-eight hours and they in turn will inform families as necessary. I must emphasise that serious disciplinary action up to and including dismissal and loss of pension rights will follow any contravention of anything I have said so far, including use of mobiles. Those of you with serious and reasonable doubts may speak to myself or any of these officers you see before you. But, and again I emphasise this, you will not be excused CB until end-ops. In a few moments I shall explain why.'

As the SFOs went round the rows issuing the portable radios, Sam and the other senior officers turned over the whiteboards. On the reverse were instructions for each group: Drugs Squad, Vice Squad and Marine Police. As far as Vic could see, none of them applied either to him and Cromer or the SFOs, and the nearest Eype came to being mentioned was the last line on the Marine Police whiteboard: 'MAINTAIN WATCH SEA AREA PORTLAND'.

'Assume the mushroom position, John.'

'For the shit that is about to befall.'

'Exactly.'

The SFOs passed out the heavy black metal portables.

Sam said, 'Now for the reason why. I shall stick to the old-fashioned Aim-Objective-Method and leave Steve Humphries to his Double-Eye-Mac system. Now – eyes down, look in.'

Sam said the aim was to take out, bang up or otherwise neutralise not one, not two, not three, but *four* armed and dangerous criminal clans or gangs. The objective was to achieve this aim without harm to the general public. One dead or injured civilian and it'd be POLICE BRUTALITY all over the papers and the whole job would be down the chute. Methods would be explained separately to each group, Drugs, Vice and Marine, by his colleagues. Sam said he hoped that was clear and pressed the remote control. He looked relieved when one of the projector screens illuminated:

ZEMUN + SHQIPERI   POSSES + MAFIYA

He took the telescopic pointer from Steve Humphries – 'Thank you, Inspector' – and tapped each word in turn. The Zemun, he said, were Serbs. Originally a clandestine assassination unit for Milosevic, led by secret police but manned by criminals, they organised and ran the Serbian drugs business. This business was estimated to be worth £10 million a month, but in addition, Serbia was a main redistribution centre for Afghani and Golden Triangle heroin bound for Europe and the UK.

Sam's pointer tapped the middle item. The 'Shkipperee', as Sam was reliably informed it was pronounced, were the Albanians. According to Met and National figures the Albanians already ran 80 per cent of the vice game in London, were rapidly expanding their brand of enforced prostitution throughout the UK, and were, of course, front runners in the illegal immigrant racket from which their supply of human flesh was derived. Some estimates ran as high as 100,000 young men and women turning over between £400 and £700 a week – *each*.

'Two hundred million pounds a month. All of it going to pimps. Enough to corner the entire UK illegal drugs market.'

The pointer moved again. Opposing these two

groups, he said, were the posses and the Mafiya. Posses needed no introduction. They were the Caribbean-led, Colombian-fed drugs gangs operating in every major UK city, and were, as of this very moment, spreading out into small towns and villages through the countryside. Marijuana originally, then cocaine, then crack, and now a useful, and growing, slice of the heroin market were in the remit of the various posses up and down the UK. Sam's pointer tapped the last name on the screen. The Mafiya had originated in Russia, mainly Moscow, Moldova and the Ukraine. They'd made their money from the break-up of the various Communist monopolies, then shipped their millions out to places like New York and London where they were happily money-laundering their way to respectability. Like the rest, the Mafiya regarded drugs as a legitimate business opportunity. These four groups, Sam said, were what they were up against.

'As if we didn't have enough with our home-grown junk-dealers and villains, now we've got these two mobs. And they're determined to fight it out, to the death, for control of the entire UK drugs supply. Let me show you what's involved –'

He pressed the remote again. A graph appeared showing world trade in billions: first was oil, second was armaments, and third, running second close, was drugs.

'Illegal drugs, ladies and gentlemen. Wasting the world's youth, wrecking the world's economies and riddling every legitimate law-abiding organisation on this planet – not excluding our own – with corruption.' He switched off the projector and leaned forward on his thick red hands. 'Now – nothing I can do or say will stop this tide any more than that old bugger Canute could, but what it will do is send a message to these foreign gentlemen that we're not the bloody soft touch they sodding well seem to think we are. This is our chance. We fail and, mark my words, we shall have war on the streets in every town and city throughout the UK. Thank you –'

Sam handed the pointer to Steve Humphries and sat down. His fellow officers applauded him. Some of the audience joined in.

28

Steve Humphries stood up. 'As Sam said, what we're looking at here is war, and that is how I intend to treat this operation.'

Vic said, 'Bit fucking gung-ho, John.'

'As per fucking usual.'

Humphries pressed both remotes. 'I-I-M-A-C' came up on one screen, an aerial photograph of Poole Freight Park on the other.

'Information – Intention – Method – Admin – Comms.' He picked up the pointer. 'Information. According to MI6, Interpol and MI5, the Mafiya have contracted with persons unknown but probably their Afghani suppliers to ferry a load of heroin across Euroland by container wagon. The target wagon has been tracked to the Cherbourg area but has now gone to ground.'

Vic said, 'In other words they've lost it.'

Humphries moved the pointer. 'Intention. Their intention is to bring the heroin over here on the Poole–Cherbourg ferry and trade or exchange it with a load of cocaine from a loose association of posses known as the North London Brothers. The Method will be to make this "smack-for-crack" exchange at a safe house known to both parties. The location of this safe house is thought to be within the Poole area.'

Vic said, 'Something else they don't know.'

'The reason for this is that both sides are looking for a quick in and out, preferably in the sort of urban environment they are familiar with, and neither side wants to be sitting on a large pile of Class A prohibited for any longer than necessary. A further complication is that the Zemun and the Shqiperi – the Serbs and Albanians, that is – have got to know about this shipment and the smack-for-crack deal it involves. Their intention is to lay their hands on both the heroin and cocaine. By armed force if necessary. Our intention is to insert a series of very large spanners into all their works. Earlier information that the shipment would be brought over in a small boat or boats has now been superseded, although in a fluid and rapidly moving situation it remains an outside possibility which will continue to be monitored. That concludes it on Information and Intention. Clear so far?'

Vic said, 'That's it then. Eype's down the pan –'

Cromer said, 'I told you –'

'However, all these parties being armed, danger-ous, and above all not terribly British, they could severally be planning to slot each other and knob off with the sweeties.' Humphries moved the pointer to the aerial photograph of the Freight Park: 'So, in case of any action occurring within the confines of the Freight Park, we've got our own fisheye cameras here as well as their security CCTV. We've also got an eye-in-the-sky helicopter back-up . . . Now any normal sane person being followed by a paraffin parrot with infrared heat-seekers turning him into a traceable white blob on the ground would immediately break off engagement and FOE. For the benefit of any ladies present, that's mobspeak for fuck-off-elsewhere –'

'Fucking loves it, doesn' he?'

'Creep.'

'As you can see the Freight Park is en route and adjacent to the ferry terminal. Buses and foot passengers could be crossing, drivers could be in their cabs kipping. Also in the Freight Park – vehicles and cargoes worth several million pounds. All only too happy to sue us. So no firefight in the Freight Park. What we do is follow the target vehicle, establish the meet, sweep the plot, get you all ground-assigned to your positions, then assuming no cock-up or major clusterfuck, it'll be Game On and across the pavement for myself and the men in black. The rest of you will remain in support until called on to clean up the plot and attend to such Blaggers, Targets and Zulus as may be left after sort-out. That's all from me. Your team leaders will now download Admin and Comms procedures.'

'Knows all the words, John.'

'Knows fuck-all else.'

As the Drugs, Vice and Marine personnel herded round their respective whiteboards, Steve Humphries and his SFO sergeant pushed through the grey plastic chairs to Vic and Cromer.

Humphries said, 'Good news –'

Vic said, 'Be the day –'

'You two get to wear the black coveralls.'

Cromer said, 'Hooray fuck.'

Humphries forced a grin. 'These two are what is known as comedians, Sergeant.'

'Yes sir. Fact noted sir.'

'Sergeant Binnegar will issue your pink slips.'

29

The Focus RS was in a holding park full of other unregistered Fords. They were two rows back from the chainlink fence separating them from the Freight Park. Behind them lay a feeder lane and unlocked access gates. Vic looked out over acres of desolate sodium-lit hardstanding. Potholes here and there had been filled with soft black tarmac which was already rutted by forty-ton trucks and trailers. Orange light shone on the dull protective wax of the Fiestas in front of them.

'Good night to nick a new motor, John. All gates open and Force Four told to fuck off home.'

Cromer was fiddling with his new Glock 19. 'What did he say about these things?'

'You were there weren't you?'

'I was for the pink-slip firearms issue. Then that armourer guy said fetch these fucking bollock-protectors.' Cromer shifted the heavy-duty Kevlar chest-to-groin shield sideways. 'How are you supposed to piss? Fucking thing makes you feel like a fucking tortoise –'

'You won't say that if it stops one.'

Cromer held out the black polycarbonate-bodied

Glock 19. 'Safety catch doesn't want to do anything.'

'You got a mag in?'

'Course –'

'Fucking hell – give it here –'

Cromer passed the Glock 19 over butt-first. Vic disengaged the selector at the left rear of the slide. 'It's not a safety, you pillock – Glocks don't have a normal safety –'

'I know the Glock 17 doesn't – but this fucker's new –'

'It's still the same basic mechanism – you can't fire it by accident because the trigger, the pin and the mag are all interlink-protected – you can throw it against the fucking wall and it won't go off. Only way it'll fire is with a five-pound trigger pull –'

'So what's that thing on the left then?'

'That, my son, engages fully automatic fire. You can get the whole nineteen shots off in a couple of seconds –'

'Fucking hell –'

'Yeah, and you were pissing about with it. Armourer said it was enough to cut a man in half.'

Cromer grinned.

Time passing like glue then radio crackle. Vic came out of his doze and thumbed the Press-To-Talk switch. Humphries' voice said, 'Alpha One, Gamma Two.'

'Go ahead Alpha One.'

'Ferry docked and target wagon to Customs. As

briefed, will be checked not searched and directed park D1.'

'Understood Alpha One.'

'Gamma Two, Gamma Three from jump-off to LUP –'

'Come again, Alpha One?'

'Get out the fucking car and on to your lying-up point.'

'Understood, Alpha One.'

'Thank God for that.'

The radio went dead.

Vic slung the black nylon bag over his shoulder. 'Don't forget the fucking keys, John –'

'You my fucking mother or what?'

Bent double they ran through the lines of cars to the gates, slid back the bolt, eased through and reset the galvanised padlock to look closed. Still crouching they ran for a rusting old container dumped next to the perimeter fence halfway down the Freight Park. Vic gave the multi-lock door two double thumps with the back of his leather-gloved fist.

A Scots voice said, 'Who?'

'Gamma Two, Gamma Three.'

The newly greased metal door slid open an inch or so. The under-barrel torch of a Heckler and Koch MP5 carbine circled over Vic and Cromer. The Scots voice said, 'You the cunts with the wire?'

Vic said, 'We fucking better be.'

Inside, the walls and floor of the container ran with

condensation. It was pitch-black except for threads of sodium-orange light raying out from three quarter-inch spyholes drilled in the container walls. Two other black-clad balaclava'd forms sat on straw bales looking out through the spyholes over the orange-lit expanse of the Freight Park.

Cromer gagged and swallowed down bile. 'What's that smell?'

The Scots voice said, 'What fucking smell?' The guy sounded edgy, pissed-off, looking for an argument.

Vic said, 'Like something's gone bad in here.'

The Scots voice said, 'Well it's not us cunts so it must be youse cunts.'

A South London voice said, 'Was a meat wagon. Till the beef crisis. Haulier went bust – it's been here ever since –'

A Welsh voice said, 'The maggots is very tasty mind.'

The Scots voice said, 'You can stand up against the wall or sit down on the floor. Either way you're gonna get a wet arse.'

'Thanks,' said Cromer.

Half an hour passed, then another burst of static. Vic saw the Scots guy thumb the PTT switch on his personal radio. Humphries' voice said, 'Alpha One, Omega Three.'

'Go go, Alpha One.'

'Target wagon through Customs, two players in

cab –'

'Omega Three Alpha One, we have eyeball.'

'You have ID, Omega Three?'

'Hang on, Alpha One . . . Left-hand-drive Volvo fridge rig, red and white bodyline, lettered "Superfrigo Pescatore" –'

'That's the one, Omega Three. Wiremen to final assault position and maintain obbo, radio silence.'

'Omega Three out.'

The Scots guy gave Vic a tap on the shoulder. 'See her?'

Vic put his eye to the quarter-inch hole. The cold night air blurred his vision.

'I said d'you fucking see her?'

Vic wiped his eye with his glove. A wall of white-painted alloy passed in front of him, then drew forward again as the driver made a pig's ear of slotting the container trailer into position. Then a string of red and white streamlined letters:

SUPERFRIGO PESCATORE

The truck stopped with a jerk and a hiss of air brakes. A plume of condensation rose from the refrigeration plant behind the truck's roof. Vic turned to the Scots guy: 'She's in the wrong slot – driver's made a right bollocks of it –'

'What the fuck –?'

'They're too close. We were told D1 – they're in D3.'

'Holy fuck.'

Another hiss of air brakes, a burst of black diesel from the upright exhaust stack and the truck drew forward out of sight.

The Scots voice said, 'Boss orders radio silence an' now the whole job's going to fucking ratshit –'

'Hang on –'

'What a fucking clusterfuck –'

'He's backing again. Trying to anyway –'

Vic watched the driver of the SUPERFRIGO truck heave the wheel-knob on to full lock. Loose black tarmac scrunched and ridged up under the wheels as the driver wound off the lock and corkscrewed the trailer into space D1. There was now a good fifteen yards between their container and the refrigerated truck.

The Scots voice said, 'Thank fucking Christ –'

The Welshman at the front of the container said, 'Second wagon approaching.'

The Scots voice said, 'That's your fucking cover –'

The second wagon had a blue and orange trailer lettered FRUITS MERIDIONALES. The rig slid easily into position and its air brakes hissed. Vic put his eye to the hole. The MERIDIONALES container was now no more than half a dozen yards away. Three or four strides and they'd be there: behind the MERIDIONALES container and on their way to the SUPERFRIGO target. Vic stood up and slung the black nylon bag on to his back.

Outside the container Cromer pulled his balaclava

down and started to move for the perimeter fence a couple of yards away. Vic held him back. 'Not yet John.'

'Eh?'

'Listen.' The rumble of a third wagon approaching. 'They're bound to watch him park up, if only to take the piss . . . When he starts, we go.' Cromer nodded. They heard the wagon stop, and double-declutch into reverse. 'Now.'

On all fours they crept round the back of the MERIDIONALES container. The third wagon was still reversing its black and yellow KELLERBRAU trailer into one of the spaces opposite. They had six yards to go across open concrete and tarmac. There was a fringe of grass and weeds along the edge of the wire-mesh fence. 'Belly-crawl John. Stay on the grass.'

'Grass is full of guard-dog shit –'

'Got gloves on haven't you?'

Vic waited, watching the mirrors and doors of the SUPERFRIGO cab: any sign of a face in a mirror and he'd know Cromer had been spotted.

When Cromer made it to the SUPERFRIGO trailer, he got to his knees, gave Vic the thumbs-up. Hampered by the bag, his Kevlar protector scraping on the broken tarmac under the grass, Vic made an awkward jungle-crawl across the gap between the trailers. Cromer was grinning through the mouth-slit in his balaclava.

'What?'

'Not exactly fucking Spiderman are you?'

'Bag doesn' help – probably smashed the fucking thing.'

He laid the bag on the gravel and peeled back the Velcro strap. Inside, still intact, three items, individually Sellotaped in bubblewrap: a ten-foot length of black wire aerial with black plastic-sheathed terminals, a black battery case the shape of a VHS cassette, and a wired black-domed tracking device with a powerful magnet on its flat underside.

'Anybody comes when I'm underneath, you're gonna have to slot the bastards because I'm gonna have my fucking hands full –'

'Supposed to shout "Armed Police", aren't we?'

'Shout what you fucking like but slot 'em.'

Cromer grinned. 'Be a pleasure.'

Vic repacked the bag, minus the bubblewrap, lay on his back and began to heave and squirm himself under the low black channel section designed to stop car drivers decapitating themselves in a pile-up. He lifted up a gloved hand and brushed out the mud and oily grit from the steel. So far so good. He taped the end of the transmitter wire inside the U-section and led the other end of the black wire forward and taped it and the battery box on top of the chassis rail. By now his balaclava was soaked in oil and grit, and, even more of a bastard, so were his gloves. He laid the dome-shaped tracker on his chest and peeled off first one glove, then the other.

Connecting the tracker, he wriggled forward, carrying it in his right hand and using his left to pull himself forward until he was under the truck's rear axle. Low foreign voices and Turkish-sounding music came from the cab above. Heart thudding, chest heaving, he hauled himself up one-handed. His whole upper body, hung on one arm, shook with muscle-tension.

Sweat and grease running into his eyes, he slid his right hand up and groped around the top of the differential housing. According to the instructions there was supposed to be a flat inspection plate secured with four domed nuts on top of the spherical housing. His fingers thick with grease, he explored the area by touch. With his arm fully outstretched and his back quivering under the strain, he found the plate, wiped it as best he could and held the tracker over it. He could feel the magnet pulling and then, while it was still an inch above the plate, it was sucked out of his fingers. Checking, he found the magnetic force made the tracker impossible to budge. Relieved, aching, and pouring with sweat, he inched backwards from the truck and lay exhausted on the tarmac under the container.

Drips of ammoniac-smelling water began to rain on his face.

The hum of a refrigeration system cutting in.

He felt rather than heard the engine start up.

He turned his head sideways and flattened his arms wide. Sharp gravel bit into the side of his balaclava'd face. Forty tons of trailer-container began to roll over him.

Oh please God not like this –

Then the low-slung channel section caught under the bottom edge of his Kevlar protector and began to lift and drag him head-first through the gravel and broken tarmac –

Shite –

Cromer's heavy bulk fell on his legs. He felt his back, all his joints stretching, cracking, then Cromer's voice – 'Hold on, Vic –'

'It's stuck under the protector – cut the fucking thing –'

The weight eased as Cromer grabbed hold of the channel section and let that bear his weight. Now both of them were being dragged along: 'Cut the fucking thing John!'

'– Think I'm trying to do?'

'Christ sake be careful – that's my bollocks under there!'

He felt the Spyderco knife rip through the coverall and cut the straps of the Kevlar protector. It scraped up over his chest and face – then it was gone and he was lying flat and still as the bottom of the channel section grazed over the side of his balaclava'd head.

'All right – you all right?'

'Better than I fucking was – thanks mate.'

'Roll back to the fence or they'll fucking see us –'

They lay half on top of each other in a smell of grass, diesel and dogshit. Vic could feel Cromer's heart pumping as hard as his own. Cromer had his glove off and was sucking blood and oil off a cut on his finger. Vic watched the LHD Volvo pull the SUPERFRIGO trailer forward and start to make a left turn towards the exit lane.

Thank Christ for that –

'Come on John, back to the ranch.'

'Fucking Spydercos –'

'What?'

'Try to close the bastards, they cut your fucking hand off.'

As they elbowed-and-kneed their way back along the fence, Vic saw the Kevlar protector rocking on the gravel. It looked like a disembowelled tortoise – with a length of black wire sticking up out of it –

Oh shit – they'd cut the transmitter wire –

To give himself more room to make the turn into the exit lane the driver of the SUPERFRIGO rig tried to back up the trailer – now he had it weaving all over the place –

'Fuck.'

'What?'

Before Vic could draw Cromer's attention to the black wire, the double rear wheels of the SUPERFRIGO trailer rolled back at an angle and crushed the chest-to-groin protector into the tarmac. When the rig pulled forward all that was left was an ellipse of black shards and a flattened loop of black transmitter wire –

Cromer grinned and said, 'That could've been you mate.'

'Yeah.' Vic stuck out his hand. 'Thanks John.'

*

Back in the container the Scots guy said, 'Christ man, you smell like a Paris fucking pissoir.'

'Fish lorry, wasn't it?'

'Anyway, they're no' getting a fucking signal so you fucked up. The boss says follow it –'

Cromer said, 'For Christ sake, look at the state of him. He was practically fucking crushed to death –'

'I don't give a fuck son. The boss says follow, you fucking follow –'

'Fuck off –'

'Leave it John –'

Radio crackle and a woman's voice cut in: 'All units, all units, Port Police. Two suspect males, Ukrainian origin but carrying French national identity cards, found dead in cabin five-one-two, freight drivers' section. Cause of death confirmed as severed trachea, temporal and carotid arteries. More follows –'

Vic said, 'Sounds as if our throat-slitting friends are back in business.'

The Scots guy looked at them. 'What the fuck –?'

'They've nicked the heroin. No wonder he couldn't drive the fucking thing. Come on, John –'

30

Vic said, 'Looks like Albania one, Ukraine nil.'

'Yeah. So much for cross-Channel security.'

'All these guys had to do was watch the ports —'

'Our lot said the wagon had gone to ground —'

'Yeah, but it's still got to queue up for the ferry. That can take the best part of a day – and it's all in the open, cars one side, lorries the other. Anybody could spot it –'

'Got to be sure they've got the right one, haven't they? It could have been registered anywhere.'

'Was me, I'd've walked the freight queue, looked in the cabs for newspapers, porno mags – aren't going to be that many in Ukrainian or whatever it is they speak –'

'Russian, isn' it?'

'Whatever – anyway, if that fails, there's always passport control. Everybody keeps their passports in their hand, John. Then there's all the lading and cargo checks – that's all in triplicate, takes a fucking age . . . All you got to do is stand there with your eyes and ears open.'

'You've still got to get on board –'

'Foot-passenger ticket –'

'Find the cabin –'

'That's what these guys are good at, John.'

They like to know where people live –

Cromer took the RS out through the arse-end of Poole in a queue of continental wagons and trailers. They wound through narrow streets, high stone walls, windowless Customs sheds.

'Place looks like a fucking prison.'

'Yeah. Welcome to the UK.'

Vic switched the car radio to channel 75, National Firearms frequency. 'Gamma Two, Alpha One.'

Humphries' voice: 'Go go, Gamma Two.'

'Approaching main junction, railway station, Barclays roundabout. No visual contact.'

'Took your fucking time, Gamma Two.'

'Heavy freight traffic, Alpha One.'

'Take A350 east, direction Parkstone. Black cab Delta One has eyeball on target vehicle so get a fucking blat on. Range Rover gunships Delta Three, Delta Four will follow.'

'We still on Plan A, Alpha One?'

Humphries voice said, 'Just do what you're fucking told, Gamma Two, and don't fuck up this time –' A burst of static, then silence.

'He sounds nervous, John.'

'Good –'

Vic replaced the radio mic. 'Put your foot down.'

Cromer took the outside lane up the ramp past the twin Barclays towers and hung a tyre-squealing right on to the A350. Two in the morning and Parkstone was deserted. Cromer kept up a steady eighty-five and took another right on to the A338 towards Bournemouth.

'There's the cab. Pull over –'

Cromer pulled in three vehicles behind the black cab.

'Gamma Two, Delta One.'

'Go go, Gamma Two.'

'Confirm eyeball, Delta One.'

'Target vehicle four up, Gamma Two.'

Vic stuck his head out of the side window. 'Move up on the verge John. Can't see a fucking thing.'

Cromer pulled over, inside tyres thrumming on the green Cat's-eyes. In front of the black cab, an old white Merc looking yellow under the light, a dark red Rover 25, a silver BMW and a white van tailgating and flashing the Volvo truck and trailer.

'Front of the mad white-van man, Delta One?'

'You got it. Silly sod's been spooking him since Poole –'

'Stupid bastard.'

'We were thinking of tugging him.'

'Try not to, Delta One.'

'Wilco Gamma Two. Peeling off next roundabout. Best of luck.'

'Thanks mate.' Vic switched off. 'I think we can move up, John. He's got his hands full with white van man.'

'Was me I'd brakelight the fucker.'

'He daren't, dare he? Not with what he's carrying.'

'Van could still screw it up for us, Vic. You slit guys' throats, you're gonna be fucking jumpy with somebody like that prat up your arse –'

'Get up one behind the van and stay back.'

The road into Bournemouth was long, straight and tree-lined, with big houses set back on each side. Soon they were sitting behind the silver BMW and doing sixty-five between the traffic lights.

'Lot of money in Bournemouth, John.'

'Christ Vic, you don' 'alf stink.'

'That fucking fish container, pissed all over me.'

'Scots git was right. Like that cast-iron pisshouse we used to have to go to top of Blackboy Hill where you could see the buggers cottaging through the perforations. Stunk like fuck.'

'Ammonia, John. He probably had a load of skate or dogfish, couldn't be bothered to wash the fucker out between trips.'

'Yeah. Doesn't help me though does it?'

'Least I don't smell of fucking dogshit.'

The silver BMW ran a red light. Cromer pushed up close behind then fell back. 'Hang on –'

'What is it now?'

'If he was running empty, why keep putting the freezer on and off? You don't need to refrigerate heroin, do you?'

'Wouldn've thought so – look out, there he goes –'

The Volvo braked hard and without signalling took a wide right into another broad tree-lined street. The white van swerved left, brakes shrieking: he shot up the inside of the Volvo on to the kerb smack into an iron-fenced tree. Rending metal, crashing glass – the radiator bursting and spraying steam and boiling rust-coloured water all over the windscreen. Vic glanced across; the bull-necked crop-headed driver was thumping the steering wheel with his fist and swearing, unaware that his contorted face was running with blood. The BMW pulled into the side of the road and stopped.

Vic said, 'Carry on John. Justice has prevailed.'

'Place'll be swarming with woodentops any fucking minute.'

'Yeah, you're right. Pull in and keep your eyes on the wagon. If he turns off, creep up no lights.'

'What a fuck-up –'

Vic picked up the mic. 'Gamma Two, Alpha One.'

Humphries voice: 'Go go, Gamma Two.'

'Eyeball corner of Raglan and Kingsleigh –'

'He's turning again Vic –' Cromer switched off his lights and began to pull away.

'Road accident white van corner of Kingsleigh and Cranmere. Repeat Kingsleigh and Cranmere –'

Humphries' voice: 'You don't fucking stop for road accidents Gamma Two – get your fucking finger out –'

'Not stopped, Alpha One. Have eyeball Raglan Road. Need to keep local plod well off plot.'

A pause, then: 'Thank you, Gamma Two. Will do. Out.'

'Where is he, John?'

'Went off second left.'

'Drive past, I'll give it a looksee.'

Raglan Crescent was broad, leafy, curved and short, with a NO THROUGH ROAD sign at the entrance. Vic turned to Cromer. 'Park up facing this way.'

They left the RS and headed back to Raglan Crescent on foot.

There was no sign of the Volvo truck and trailer.

Vic said, 'Can't go in like this – we look like fucking blaggers.'

Cromer said, 'Got my civvies in the boot –'

'A jacket'll do. Keep into the hedges.'

Vic moved himself into the cover of the fourteen-foot rhododendron bushes and waited. On each corner of the cul-de-sac stood large Tudor-style houses: fretted white gables, black beams, ornamental brickwork and diamond-paned double bay windows. No lights in either house. He heard Cromer open and close the boot of the RS. Even though he did it quietly, and you had to be listening for it, somewhere a dog woofed. Deep, like a German shepherd –

Oh Jesus, not fucking dogs –

Silence. Vic could smell dust and pine needles. Cromer came padding up in a dark tweed jacket. 'Dog around somewhere, John.'

'Yeah. I heard.'

'Looks like the two gardens each side stretch right back. Gates locked and no sign of the wagon. Sure it was this turning?'

'Course I'm fucking sure.'

'Got to be another big joint down the bottom then. Round the curve —'

'Yeah.'

'Somewhere behind all them fucking pines and rhododendrons. Some nursing home or something. Christ knows we've passed enough.'

'Yeah, whole place is fucking geriatric.'

'Don't go a lot on street lighting do they?'

'No.'

'Magged up?'

Cromer checked the Glock 19. 'Seated.'

'Off you go then.'

Vic lost sight of Cromer as he bent double round the curve. He moved deeper into the dusty dead rhododendrons and checked his own Glock 19.

Automatic off. Magazine seated. Low grey sky. A sodium and mercury vapour glare to the south, on the sea front. No traffic. No cars on the streets. No noise. No fuck-all. It was what these people paid for . . .

He thought of Ellie. She'd be sound asleep at Joe's now, well fed, well looked after, lying in bed, one arm flung out across the pillow —

For fuck's sake Hallam, what are you worried about?

He checked the Glock again, tapping the foot of the mag with the heel of his hand. He'd noticed everybody did that when they were out on a weapons job: you waited, you checked the kit over and over. Five minutes later you did it again. Making sure —

Cromer appeared, crouched and loping, his

rubber-soled para boots making no sound on the speckled asphalt. A manic grin and he was punching Vic's shoulder. Vic could smell his hot fresh adrenalin sweat. 'Fucking scored mate! We've fucking scored!'

31

The driver's door on the four-ton armoured Range Rover opened. DS Binnegar said, 'It's bandit glass and it don't wind down. Get in the back.'

Vic and Cromer watched the two fully kitted-up assaulters climb out of the back seats. In their ballistic helmets, goggle-eyed respirators, elbow pads, leg guards and carrying retractable-stock MP5 sub-machine guns, they looked more like starship troopers than coppers. Once out they ran silently to take up obbo positions at the end of Raglan Crescent. Vic and Cromer climbed in. The Range Rover smelled of sweat and gun oil.

Humphries said, 'For Christ sake don't slam the fucking door.' He twisted round in his seat and stared at Vic. 'So, what have we got? Anything?'

'Show him, John.'

Cromer passed forward a torn-out sheet from his notebook. 'This is the layout.'

Humphries held the lined paper between his knees under the shielded map light. 'How accurate?'

'I paced it. Side to side, front to back.'

'I hope you didn't go right up to the fucking house.'

'No sir.' Cromer leaned forward and moved his

finger along the bottom of the ballpoint drawing. 'There's a line of Cupressus here at the front edge of the car park. I used that for cover.'

'The fuck's Cupressus?'

'Cypress. Leylandii. A fast-growing hedge material. Sir –'

Humphries shot him a don't-smartarse-me look. 'Thirty-five-yard frontage?'

'Give or take a yard.'

'Big.' Humphries glanced at DS Binnegar. 'Too big for eight of us.'

Binnegar said, 'We've got two ARVs coming up.'

'How many on?'

'A dozen Authorised Firearms Officers, two drivers.'

'Most of these so-called AFOs couldn't hit a bag of shit with a shovel.' He looked over his shoulder at Vic and Cromer. 'Still, we've always got these two fucking comedians, haven't we?'

Vic said, 'Yes sir. You have.'

Humphries pointed to one of the rectangles Cromer had drawn in the front car-park area. 'What's this?'

'That's the sign, sir. "Raglan School of English. Tourism Business Professional."'

'How many spaces in the car park?'

'Eight, sir. But the truck is one side, the trailer the other. As I have indicated, sir, with the larger rectangles.'

'So you have. Doors, windows?'

'Double entrance doors off centre. Wooden, wrought-iron studded –'

Humphries looked across to Binnegar. 'Bastard.'

'Windows, one double bay left, single bay right. Both leaded lights, stone mullions –'

'Bastard.'

'Three more windows along each side sir, double glazed as far as I could see. Two kitchen-type doors, wire-mesh glass, one each side –'

'This car park. Tarmac or gravel?'

'Gravel sir.'

'And the paths each side of the house?'

'The same.'

'Fuck. Not making it easy for us are they, Sarge?'

Binnegar said, 'No sir.'

Humphries said, 'What about upstairs?'

Cromer said, 'Four across the front, sir. Two over the double bay, one over the single. All leaded lights, stone mullions. As is the oriel over the staircase, sir.'

'What the fuck's an oriel?'

'Projecting bay window, sir. Supported by corbels –'

Humphries breathed heavily. 'You're a pretty smart kiddie all around, aren't you? Handy with a piece too, by all accounts –'

'Yes sir, thanks to you –'

Vic kicked Cromer's ankle.

Humphries said, 'Well don't get too fucking smart with me, understand?'

'Yes sir.'

'Good. How far from front to back?'

'Twenty yards, sir, with a grass verge and three double-glazed bedroom windows each side.'

'Then what?'

'A full-width south-facing glass conservatory, central stone patio, three circular steps to the lawn, flowered borders, another Cupressus hedge, ten-foot brick wall to the rear with an arched wooden door to the right leading to Cardigan Avenue.'

'You should've been a fucking estate agent.'

'Thank you sir.'

Humphries gazed at Cromer's sketch for a full minute. Then he turned to Binnegar. 'Have the houses each side been told?'

'Yes sir.'

'Who by?'

'Local plod. It was thought better, since the occupants would be more familiar with their uniform than ours, sir.'

'Fucking right. What happened?'

'They agreed to go to their basements, wine cellars, whatever.'

'They'll be well fixed then.'

'Should be.'

'They offer us a cuppa?'

'No sir.'

'Typical.'

'They don't want us in their houses either, sir.'

'Why?'

'Carpets and furniture mostly, sir –'

'Poxy rich cunts are all the same. Mean as fuck.'

'Case of what we have we hold, sir.'

Humphries waved Cromer's sketch in the air: 'Where the fuck am I going to brief twenty-odd men with this piece of shit?'

'Local plod said they could duplicate it sir.'

'How?'

'Local plod shop sir.'

'Still leaves where.'

'House on the right said we could have their garage.'

'What about their precious fucking Roller or whatever?'

'They have two garages sir. We can have the one with the mowers in.'

'Fucking stroll on.' Humphries shoved the sheet of notepaper at Binnegar. 'Here. Tell the driver to go slow, no lights, until he's out on the main road then get a fucking blat on.'

'Will do, sir.'

'Get the team in so we can kick the job around.'

'Will do –'

As Binnegar slipped out of his seat Humphries turned to Vic and Cromer. 'And you two can fuck off as well.'

They had twenty minutes' doze in the RS, then the radio: 'All units Savernake Lodge. Left-hand garage, repeat, left-hand garage. Try not to walk on the lawns, owners don't like boot marks on the stripes.'

It was a large double garage, strip-lit and

dehumidified, with a pair of ride-on mowers and various Flymos, strimmers, trimmers and gardening tools neatly racked on the whitewashed brick walls.

Binnegar was on the door handing out duplicates of Cromer's sketch. Humphries stood at the far end with his team of eight kitted-up assaulters sitting on their Bergens in front of him. The rest of the Vice and Drugs AFOs in plainclothes except for their chequered POLICE baseball caps either sat on the flagstoned floor or lounged against the toolracked walls. Vic and Cromer leaned against the automatic up-and-over garage door.

Humphries said, 'As you should all know by now, two men thought to be Ukrainian hostiles were slotted on the ferry. All this means is that the Zemun and the Albanians, or Shqiperi or whatever they choose to call themselves, think they're nicely settled in their own safe house and several leagues ahead of the game. We're here to prove they're not. Now listen up –'

He went straight into his briefing. There would be front and rear containment, he said, with one Armed Response Vehicle blocking the car-park entrance, and the other parked close up on the pavement to blank off the arched garden door to Cardigan Avenue. Each ARV would contain one armed AFO and driver supplied with three-foot stave or similar from the ARV bang box.

'That leaves us with twenty men, and two dogs –'

Vic said, 'Looks like we're out the loop, John –'

'Thank fuck for that –'

'DS Binnegar will lead his stick of four assaulters through the back garden door to the conservatory. I shall take my stick of four through the front doors and create as much fuck in the ancestral hall as necessary to secure the staircase and rooms each side. The eight AFOs remaining will position themselves along the side paths opposite windows and doors. You will use Remington 870 pumpguns with "Ferret" CS gas cartridges and powdered lead-and-wax Hatton rounds. Your job is to CS the side-bedrooms and blow the hinges off the side doors with the Hattons. You will not, repeat not, enter the plot under any circumstances. Otherwise we shall have crossed arcs of fire and general all-out clusterfuck. Finally, let me remind you of Section Three, the key words of which are "Such Force As May Be Necessary". In other words we are not out to slot these fuckers or whoever else may be in the building. We are here to petrify their fucking arses with all the firepower at our disposal but excluding, hopefully, live rounds. You understand? We want them to come out shitting themselves, not shooting. On the other hand, if any one of the silly fuckers is still carrying once asked not to, feel free to slot him. My assaulters will be wearing respirators and helmets. These cut down all-round vision by fifty per cent so try not to get in their way because you could end up shot. Radio earpieces in now please. The next voice you hear will be mine. When I say "Go, go, go!" it'll be Game On and we shall be across the pavement. From you I shall want to hear the Battle of fucking Alamein. Thank you.'

As Humphries and Binnegar moved out with the eight assaulters, Vic said, 'Anything for us?'

Humphries said, 'Yeah. Blag some boltcutters and secure that fucking trailer container. Think you can do that?'

'We'll try.'

'How very kind.'

32

'Go, go, go!'

Vic and Cromer followed Humphries and his four-man stick at a swerving run across the car park. The deep repeated bark of pump-action shotguns echoed round the house. Cordite and an acrid, throat-catching smell. Vic and Cromer veered off right to the container. Down the right side of the house they could see gouts of orange flame stabbing up towards the bedrooms. Glass burst, crashed and tinkled on to gravel. Humphries and the Method-Of-Entry man leapt up the steps to the doors. Covered by Humphries' ballistic shield, the MOE man set the electro-hydraulic ram against the doors. A low whirr, then hardened steel teeth bit into the oak. Two assaulters took out the downstairs windows and hurled in flash-bang stun grenades. The concussion was tremendous, deep and chest-shaking even at a distance. Showers of fragmented glass and smoking curtain blew out of the windows. Billows of blackish-green smoke followed. The heavy oak doors began cracking under the four-ton-per-square-inch pressure. Backing up the first two assaulters, the third man blasted the double bay bedroom then the single bay with a Remington 870 loaded with 'Ferret' CS gas. The MOE man had unslung his sawn-off 870 and was pumping lead-and-wax Hatton rounds into the wrought-iron strap-hinges. The doors sagged, and swung apart on the remains of their top straps. The ram clanked down on to the brick steps and the assaulters stacked up on the doors. Humphries raised his shield and threw in a flash-bang then a ten-shot rapid.

'First man in!' The MOE man charged through the doors, with Humphries on his shoulder, shield in one hand, MP5 in the other. The MOE man dashed right, Humphries dumped the shield, ducked left, pulled a stun grenade from his belt rig and slung it along the black and white tiled floor.

BLAAM!

For a second a carved-oak staircase was lit stark white then it was gone and blackish smoke was boiling out and Humphries was yelling, 'Second man right! Third man left! Fourth man stairs!' As they piled in, the doors fell flat under their charge and another rolling ball of smoke whooshed out. The under-barrel Maglites on their MP5s raked and stabbed the dark. Grenades and ten-shot rapids flashlit the rooms on either side. The whole ground floor boomed, shook with dust and filled with smoke. Shouts of 'Room clear!' 'Room clear!' echoed in their earpieces, then a few seconds' silence, and Humphries' voice shouted, 'Downstairs clear! Outside units cease firing!'

*

Whitish CS gas began seeping out of the smashed upper windows. It had seemed like an everlasting ear-splitting bombardment, but when Vic glanced at his watch he saw it had taken less than thirty seconds.

Humphries and the MOE man ran out on to the steps. Humphries pulled his respirator aside. The MOE man passed him a loudhailer mic on a coiled lead and pointed the bullhorn at the shattered upper windows. Humphries bellowing, 'In the house! Armed Police!'

Vic caught the flash of reflected light from a Velux window pushing open in the vee between the twin gables. A thick bundle of towels appeared, then another. A bare brown arm and a glint of metal –

'Alpha One – on the roof!'

Humphries and the MOE man turning to locate Vic's shout –

Two men, in bluish-white vests and Y-fronts, heads wrapped in bathroom towels against the CS, were climbing out on to the guttering between the gables. Both were carrying, belly-crawling to the roof valley's edge –

Vic thumbed his PTT and screamed, 'Alpha One, Gamma Two! On the fucking roof!'

Humphries and the MOE man diving flat and scrabbling over the herringbone brick steps for the doorway –

Stabs of red fire, the thunderous hammer-blatter of a pair of Uzi automatics –

Bullets kicking up a spray of red chips round their feet –

The MOE man howling, curling up, clutching his ankle –

Cromer lying flat at the corner of the container, sighting up at the roof along the barrel of his Glock – getting off a two-second full-mag burst – turning and grinning at Vic –

More screams –

Vic hauling back on Cromer's legs pulling him behind the container –

WHANG!

Bullets sprayed, whirred and ricocheted all along the door face of the container. Cromer was struggling to reload, writhing to get free. Vic pulled his Glock and brought the butt down hard on Cromer's wrist. The gun fell in the gravel. Vic kicked it away and dragged Cromer's arm up behind his back.

'What the fuck –?'

'You mad fucker!'

'What –?'

'He's just waiting for you to stick your fucking head out!'

Vic threw a handful of gravel out past the end of the container. Another hammering burst from the Uzi and the spray of bullets smacked into the gravel at the end of the container. A yard-long gap appeared in the gravel and gouged out a smoking trench in the dusty soil beneath.

'That would've been your head, cunt.'

'Yeah . . .'

Vic felt the tension go out of Cromer. He let go his arm. Cromer sat up and leaned back against the container, breathing hard. 'Must've winged – one of the bastards – heard the fucker scream –'

'Oh yeah. One out of nineteen and he thinks he's Wyatt fucking Earp.'

Cromer grinned, then rubbed and licked his reddened wrist. 'Tell you what.'

'What?'

'Them Glocks don' 'alf come tight –'

Humphries' voice yelling, 'Casevac! Casevac!'

DS Binnegar's black-clad bulk squeezing up through the Velux, firing off unsighted double-taps to keep the dark guys' heads down, then rolling aside and heaving two other black-clad assaulters up through the Velux on to the roof.

The two dark guys in blue-white vests and Y-fronts squirming round on their stomachs to face them –

The two assaulters spidering up the roof-pitch to the shelter of the central chimneys; on their backs the scopes and spindly twin legs of their Steyer 7.62mm sniper rifles silhouetted against the black-orange sky –

A Uzi splitting chunks of brick and red dust off the spiral gingerbread stacks –

Two sharp cracks like slate breaking –

Two men in blue-white underwear knocked backwards by the double impact –

Tangling and rolling over the valley gutter's edge –

One yelling, both falling –

An untidy double thud as a mass of flailing limbs and torsos hit the brick steps –

It was over.

33

The two bodies lay where they had fallen.

Vic looked at their faces then stood back to watch Humphries' assaulters bringing out a shuffling bare-foot group of men and women. They were made to look at the bodies then lie face down in the gravel. The assaulters plasticuffed them hand and foot and stretched their arms out in front of them. Four were women in short white massage-coats. One of the men was thickset and wore grey sweat-pants, the other two were skinnier, younger, in their underwear. The assaulters stood over them, MP5s slanting at their heads. Vic walked past taking a good look at the three men. None of them had been in solitary on the *Aware*. Nor had the two dead men. Vic walked slowly back to the container. Where the fuck were the four who had escaped from the prison van?

Still out there somewhere – they had to be . . .

'Right John, let's open the box.' He took one arm of the three-foot boltcutter, handed Cromer the other. The container doors were streaked to the metal with bright dents and bullet tracks. The small bolts and padlocks fell to the gravel. Vic put the Customs seals in an evidence bag and hung it from one of the hasps. They clamped the boltcutter on to the vertical tie-rod connecting the top and bottom bolts. 'Two-six – heave –'

The half-inch tie-rod snapped, pinged and rattled round in its mounts.

They hauled open the doors – and reeled back from the musty ammoniac reek: runnels of yellow-brown water streamed over the container lip into the gravel.

'Jesus Christ –'

Glock in hand, Cromer shone his torch over the dripping walls and floors. Up at the far end was a heap of large sodden lumps. They looked like piles of hospital bagwash.

Cromer's torch moved slowly over a dozen or so female bodies. Here and there, a face, a swathe of long hair, a hand holding a plastic water bottle. Not a movement anywhere.

'Fucking hell, Vic – they're all dead –'

The beam from his torch wavered, dipped and flailed all over the place: Cromer lurched away into the hedge to throw up. Vic took a couple of steps back from the container, breathed down a lungful of fresh night air and looked over at the house.

Humphries and DS Binnegar came out, glanced at the captives, moved to one side, and loosened their respirators to talk. They looked relieved, and laughed as they exchanged remarks.

Behind them, in the open hallway, another assaulter had hung a big yellow Dragon lamp on a chair-back above the legs of the MOE man. He stuck a hypo into the MOE man's bared calf and began cutting away the laces of his para boot. Blood had pooled on the tiled floor. The intense white light from the one-million-candle-power lamp made it look black.

Humphries moved away from DS Binnegar, thumbed his PTT. 'Dogs and handlers in the house. Outside units on standby.'

Vic turned away and shone his torch into the container. Cromer staggered back from the cypress hedge, eyes watering, wiping his mouth with the back of his glove. 'Sorry about that –'

Vic switched off his Maglite, put his hand on Cromer's shoulder and levered himself up into the back of the container. Now the ammoniac smell was mixed with sweat and sickly-sweet old-fashioned deodorant. He forced himself not to gag. 'Keep your torch on 'em, John.'

'Yeah but –'

'You don't piss yourself if you're dead.'

'No but –'

'Just don't fucking shoot me, that's all.'

He flattened himself against the wall of the container and slid forward a step at a time. When he was close enough to touch the nearest inert young woman, he saw she was gaffer-taped mouth, hand and foot. He bent to cut off the wet strips of two-inch

silver insulation tape and put his fingers to her neck.
It was sheened in sweat but warm. He felt for the
pulse under her left ear: faint, rapid, fluttering –

'Get a fucking medic, John –'

'Supposed to be on standby –'

'Fuck standby, find a fucking medic –'

'Yeah but –'

'Try the ARV wagon on the gate – and run, you
fuckhead –'

He shone his torch back on them. Fifteen. Lying all
over each other. All young. Some in thin summer
dresses, some in sleeveless blouses over black slacks.
All in unfastened platform sandals. All with swollen
legs and distended stomachs. To Vic's eye they didn't
look pregnant, like Ellie: the bulge was lower – they
looked bloated, like the floaters you got in the docks –

Or that poor cow they picked up off Portland –

She'd been strapped up with two-inch silver tape –

Hang on –

That was March and this was May –

They must be bringing them over by the fucking truckload –

He got down on his hands and knees and crawled
amongst them, pushing and heaving their limp heavy
bodies apart, desperate to free their mouths from the
slimy silver tape. He dropped his torch; he made
himself plough on through the dark, feeling for their
wet hair, faces, mouths. Now and then their limbs and
torsos flopped over and pinned him down flat and
breathless, leaving him gasping and panic-stricken.

Forcing himself to breathe in deep, shoving his arms and legs through wet clothing and kicking against clammy flesh: it was, he thought, like swimming through corpses . . .

He crawled out and stood up, arms and legs shaking, trying to get his nerve and his breath back, peeling clumps of slimy silver tape from his hands and coveralls.

Christ, John – where the fuck are you?

He began to haul on their floppy-armed slippery dead weight. He had managed to drag four of them to the doorway when he heard the front gates graunch back over the gravel. The Armed Response Vehicle on front containment crawled through. It pulled round and blazed its headlamps full on into the container. He ducked his head out of the lights and sank bank on to the door lip, speechless, soaked in sweat and totally knackered.

'All right Vic – you all right?'

'Another eleven – inside – I don't know if they're all –'

He felt Cromer hauling him up under the armpits. 'Come on, mate, they got a brew on round the back.'

Vic swigged at the mug of hot sweet tea. Boots crashed on gravel. Humphries' voice: 'Who's fucking idea's this?'

Vic said, 'Mine sir –'

Cromer said, 'Mine sir –'

'I got a dozen fucking hostiles back there, maybe more in the house –'

'This was an emergency sir –'

'So you thought you'd move the whole fucking front containment?'

'Fifteen young women in there, sir – they're in a bad way –'

'So will you fucking be –'

DS Binnegar ran up, respirator flapping. 'House clear – no further bodies –'

'They find it?'

'No sir, house is clean.'

Humphries went ape. 'How can it be fucking clean? I've got two dead, one man wounded – all this *shit* –' He waved at the container: 'And you tell me the house is fucking *clean?*'

'Yes sir.'

'Where's the fucking heroin?'

'Dogs picked up a couple of grass tabs and a used cocaine wrap –'

'I don't want fucking fag-ends, Sergeant! *I want that fucking heroin!*'

'Yes sir –'

Vic swallowed a last hot gulp of tea. He pointed at the container. 'I think you'll find it's over there. Sir –'

'What?'

'The heroin. It's in those young girls. In their bellies –'

34

Humphries leaned out of the passenger door. 'You two better fuck off back double quick. Sea Scouts have been having fun and games up this Eype place of yours. Sam's in St Bride's, says where the fuck are you –' He grinned and slammed the door. The Range Rover accelerated and spat gravel at them.

Vic said, 'Thanks for fuck-all.'

Cromer said, 'I'll have that bastard one day.'

Vic said, 'Yeah. Get the RS will you?'

The plot had been handed over to local CID. Their forensic teams were everywhere, on the roof, in the house, poking round the car park, bagging and auto-flashing everything from blood samples and ammo cases to styrofoam cups and sandwich wraps. Vic walked past the container. It was empty and the green-clad paramedics were reversing their ambulances and pulling out.

Fun and games –

Cromer was doing one-twenty down the A35 dual carriageway past Poole. 'For Christ sake say something or I'll fall a-fucking-sleep.'

'You talk to the Drug and Vice guys?'

'Yeah. Place was a knocking shop –'

'Yeah. Punters had to come in the back door though.'

'Why?'

'The neighbours. Complained about the car noise.'

'Yeah. They would.' Cromer slowed for the round-about, squealed round it and sped back up to ninety along the rhododendron-lined straight. A pale brown thing bounced halfway across the road, stopped and stared, eyes as bright as mercury – then a thud.

'Watch out for the bunnies.'

'Yeah. What gets me is the local guys knew all about it.'

'Ever worked on Vice, John?'

'Done the tour down City Road. Picking up kerb-crawlers mostly –'

'Set-up like this you're on a hiding to nothing. The guys running it are all illegals anyway. You pick 'em up, some arsehole gets 'em out on bail, they fucking leg it. Off on one ferry, back on the next, new papers. Same with the girls, the witnesses. They don't want kicking out the country so they fuck off up north, like as not end up in some other knocking shop. All you're left with is a desk full of crap and no fucking case.'

Cromer pushed the RS up to a hundred and ten. The twenty-foot walls of rhododendrons whizzed by in a red and white blur. 'Guy at Winfrith said they'd closed down the trafficking squad for lack of funds.'

'Lack of interest more like.'

'You see the girls they brought out the house?'

'Not close up, no.'

'Bruises big as fucking apples all over.'

'They come over here thinking they're going to learn English – they don't realise they're going to learn it lying on their fucking backs. These guys tell the girls they owe 'em thousands for bringing 'em in. They got no papers, nothing. How else are these girls going to pay up?'

'Yeah but why punch fuck out of 'em – why damage the goods?'

'Fear, John. How these guys operate. They're not like us.'

They like to know where people live –

When they made it to the new stretch of dual carriageway after Bere Regis, Cromer had the RS flat-out at one-forty plus.

'What the medics say about the kids in the container, Vic?'

'Said they were tranked up to the eyeballs to stop them shouting and banging on the ferry. Once they're softened up, they feed 'em French letters full of heroin. One of the guys said he thought the record was ninety-eight. Kid of eleven, he said.'

'Fucking hell.'

'It's only a couple of kilos each. Three at the most. Medic said from the musty smell he thought they'd all been given Imodium and frusemide.'

'What's frusemide?'

'Makes you wet yourself.'

'Fucking hell.' Cromer wiped his palms one at a time down the legs of his black coveralls. 'Sounds fucking dodgy to me – I mean, all that palaver for thirty, forty kilos.'

'You're right, John – it is fucking dodgy.'

'I mean it's not just a matter of slitting those two on the ferry – it's Doochy, Allie, his ma, that fucking hijack up on Eggardon – all for what, a million, million half?'

'About that, yeah. Plus what they'd make off the girls. Four or five hundred quid a week each for three or four years. Then flog 'em on. Punters are always looking for fresh meat, John.'

'Still sounds a bit fucking desperate.'

'Maybe Sam was right –'

'How?'

'What he said about fucking war. Control of the whole fucking drug market. In which case there's more to come.'

Cromer kept it down to eighty along the Dorchester bypass. Vic watched him frowning and thinking to himself.

'How d'you mean, Vic, more to come?'

'I think they're aiming for Albania two, Ukraine nil. I think this is Doochy's smack-for-crack deal – only difference is the Albanians are running it. You get a surgical-steel lune at your throat, you're not going to keep your gob shut are you?'

'Doochy did.'

'Only so long as it was his game.'

'The two drivers –?'

'Could be, could be anybody. There's always somebody with a grudge, somebody who thinks they should be getting a bigger whack. As Sam said, once these fuckers start trusting each other we're bolloxed.'

'Yeah, but according to Humphries –'

'Humphries is covering his arse. He knows he's shot his load too soon. And in the wrong place. As Sam has just found out –'

'I fucking hope so –'

'I'm also thinking we could be in the shit.'

'Again?'

'Yeah. I think this is those fuckpigs out of solitary. Them and their mates. We know them – Sam wants us down there –'

'Fucking great – I only saw the fuckers once when I was going round the *Aware* –'

'They bust out of the prison van. They didn't do that for nothing. They weren't in that Raglan joint. Where are they?'

'Oh shit.'

Vic said, 'Yeah. Could be.'

Ten miles to go.

Cromer said, 'Two of those girls didn't look like they'd make it.'

'They didn't.'

'Fuck.'

'Hypothermia, suffocation, whatever. Driver kept

switching the freezer on to keep 'em quiet. You're taped up, tranked up, you're cold, you're wet, you're frightened. You can barely move so you pile up together for warmth and you pass out. Those two didn't wake up.'

'What a bastard . . . What a fucking life.'

'Not over yet, John.'

'They know where they're from?'

'Moldova, mostly.'

'Moldova?'

'Where the pretty ones come from, so they say.'

35

It had taken them forty minutes to do the sixty-odd miles. On and off Vic had been trying Ellie's mobile. All he got was the woman's voice, low and meant to be calming: *'The Vodaphone you have called is switched off. Please try later.'*

Cromer said, 'No luck?'

Vic said, 'She has to keep it off in hospital. Sometimes she forgets to switch on when she comes off duty. Nights she leaves it off until she wakes up.' He checked the RS's digital clock against his watch: coming up to half four and still dark. 'No problem.'

'You'll see her when we get there –'

'Yeah.'

Cromer glanced across. 'Not getting antsy are you?'

'No. Just knackered.' Vic pressed REDIAL.

'The Vodaphone you have called . . .'

The quay on St Bride's Harbour was a glare of white arc-lights on blue police stands. Three squad cars and a white Transit van blocked off the knuckle end of the pier. Uniformed police in shirtsleeves and body armour were stringing the area with DO NOT CROSS tape. In the Cut behind the tape lay a thirty-foot Marine Police rigid inflatable boat. The starboard flotation sponson of the RIB was punctured, its grey plasticised skin crumpled like elephant hide. Half crippled, the lopsided hull slopped about on the slick black water. The helmsman, lifejacket and body armour loosened, ballistic helmet off, slumped over the wheel, head down and exhausted.

Vic walked over to the brightly lit Harbour Café. Half four and its windows were already steamed up. As Vic pushed the door open eight Marine Police in dark blue lifejackets turned and stared. Their faces were brick-red from a combination of café-heat and weather-exposure. MP5 carbines hung from black straps over the backs of their chairs and black ballistic helmets were piled on a nearby table. Water pooled round the chairs and ran off their sea boots. At the end of the table, Sam, in a waterproof police jacket, looked up from his full English breakfast. 'Be with you as soon as I've finished this debriefing.' The Marine Police grinned at each other.

Vic took mugs of tea and bacon rolls over to Cromer. The harbour crane was hauling *Rob Roy* out of the Cut. Joe was guiding it down into its cradle of trig-stands. Both props were bent and grey water spouted out from a foot-long crack in the bow below the waterline. Joe hammered chocks in under the trig-stands. He stood up. There was no smile. 'Hallo Vic –'

Vic handed Cromer a mug of tea and a bacon roll and passed his own to Joe. 'What happened?'

'Oh, Scrump piled it up on Eype Beach –'

'How's Ellie?'

'She's with Cath. They both got up when I did –'

'They both got up?' Vic pressed REDIAL again.

'The Vodaphone you have called . . .'

'Yeah – three Marine coppers hammering and banging on the fucking door half past three in the morning. Would I come and get my boat back off Eype Beach – oh fuck, look out –'

A couple of short-haired young men in jeans and yellow-and-silver jackets ambled over. One flipped open a leather-clad ID. 'Customs and Excise. All right if we look her over, skip?'

'Bit of a mess down below. I'll come with you – got enough trouble without your lot suing me for broken legs.'

'That bad is it?'

'Worse.'

'Sorry about that. You want to see the search order?'

'No, fuck it. I'll get the ladder –'

'Thanks skip –'

Vic said, 'Joe –'

'Talk to you later Vic.' Joe propped a wooden ladder against the hull, climbed up, helped the Customs men on board and shone a torch into the wheelhouse and storage hold below.

Cromer said, 'He's really pissed off.'

Vic looked at the yellowish-white gash in the bow. 'Yeah, so am I –'

'Vic!' Sam was standing on the steps of the Harbour Café.

'I'll just try Ellie once more –'

'The Vodaphone you have called . . .'

He followed Cromer over to the café.

Sam led them into the small side room the café used as an ice-cream parlour. 'They do a bloody good breakfast in here, once you've rousted the buggers out of bed –'

'Yeah, I'll bet they love it.' Vic pulled out a chair, keyed in AUTOMATIC REDIAL and set the mobile on the grey formica table.

Sam said, 'What's that for?'

'Trying to call Ellie.'

'Fucking hell Vic – I got eight blokes next door been at sea for the last six hours, shattered and fucking shot at, and all you want to do is call your missis –'

Vic stood up, shoved his chair in. 'Look Sam, if you've got a problem with that, talk to John here and I'll fuck off now –'

Sam waited, then pushed Vic's chair back with his foot. 'All right, Vic, sit down. It's been a long night and we're all a bit fucking jumpy . . .' He watched Vic lower himself into the chair. 'I'll keep this short as I can. Okay?'

'Fine –'

'Basically what you need to know is that we've still

got up to half a dozen of these Balkanian fuckpigs on the loose. We think they're still at sea but their boat's fucked –'

Vic and Cromer exchanged glances. Vic said, 'What sort of boat?'

'One of these rigid inflatables – what do they call 'em?'

'RIBs.'

'That's it.' Sam pulled out his notebook. 'Anyway this is the rest of it, as far as I can make out from all these fucking reports and phone calls I've been getting. Ready?'

Vic nodded. Cromer took out his pocketbook and clicked his Bic.

'Right. Six o'clock yesterday morning this bloke Roger Giffen, aka Scrump, arrives Barfleur, fifteen miles east of Cherbourg. A French tractor and trailer drives up, they spend the morning loading what he describes on the dockets as fuel and food supplies. Five that afternoon he leaves, giving his destination as Portland. Twice between eight and ten that evening he's reported by a Jap car container and the Weymouth–Channel Island ferry for erratic course-keeping and danger to navigation. General consensus is the silly bugger must have flaked out at the wheel. Your mate Joe Moore reckons he was pissed. Our Marine Police clock him off Portland, radio him, no reply –'

'The Vodaphone you have called . . .'

'Can you turn that down a bit?'

Vic adjusted the volume. 'Sorry Sam –'

'No problem. Now – they're on Sea Watch Area Portland, they've got the reports from the Japs and the ferry, they know he's got a St Bride's Weymouth registration, so they send that RIB out. When the RIB sees he's heading past St Bride's and on west towards Eype, they radio back Portland Control and are told to stand off, no lights, and keep track of him on radar. Portland call me because they figure he's part of this drugs op –'

'Scrump?'

'Hang on a minute Vic –'

'Not in a million years –'

'Just listen will you?' Sam licked his thick red fingers and turned the page of his notebook. 'It's now three this morning and your mate Scrump is nudging in towards Eype Beach and taking it very very slow. Portland Control get on to the RIB and tell them to back right off because there's an unidentified inflatable coming up fast from the west over by Lyme Regis. The Marine Police RIB pulls back to the new harbour wall there –' Sam pointed out of the window to the mass of cranes, sheds, steel shuttering and blocks of masonry lining the new wall: 'They can't be picked out by radar or line of sight because of all the clutter. Apart from that, the Marine Police RIB can do over forty knots so they're only a minute or so away from Eype. By now your mate Scrump is about thirty yards offshore. Suddenly he opens up both throttles and goes flat-out for the shore like a fucking maniac – he's pushing a fucking great wall of water in front of the bows – and he shuts off dead –'

Vic said, 'He did that with us, John –'

Cromer said, 'Yeah, the stupid bastard –'

Sam said, 'What happens is, he ends up with the front end on the beach and the arse end in the water. Seconds later he's up on deck and chucking stuff on to the beach –'

Cromer looked up. 'What sort of stuff?'

'The Marine Police say plastic bales. They immediately think "fucking-hell-this-is-the-drug-drop" and set off full whack from the harbour wall. They keep their binocs on him and the next thing they see is a double orange flash from the lane off the beach, a second later they hear the double bang –'

'Shotgun?'

'Yeah, birdshot. They found the cases in the lane. So, the Marine Police put their searchlight on Scrump. He's up and off down the beach like a fucking longdog –'

'Hang on, Sam. Who's doing the shooting?'

'Coming to that. They pull the searchlight round and there's this big Mitsubishi Shogun with half a dozen black guys jumping out and legging it after Scrump. The Marine Police are closing in on the beach and the loudhailer's yelling "Armed Police! Armed Police!" The Yardies –'

Vic said, 'You sure they're Yardies?'

'They've got dreadlocks and fucking guns, Vic – they're Yardies . . . What I reckon is – these Yardies see the fucking searchlight, hear "Armed Police", figure they've been set up and Scrump's part of it, the bait in the trap. So they pull these MAC 10 fucking machine pistols they've got – twelve hundred rounds a minute, two thousand in a long mag – no more Scrump.'

'Where is he?'

'In that white van on the knuckle. Got bullets in the back of his head, his spine, his pelvis, both fucking legs. Well and truly sprayed. Dead when he hit the gravel.'

'Poor bastard.'

'Yeah.'

Cromer said, 'They get any of 'em?'

'No. The fuckers were back in the Shogun and away. Patrol car found the Shogun in the Eype pull-in off the bypass.'

Vic said, 'They find any coke in it?'

'Clean as a whistle. Handlers had dogs all over it.'

'So much for Doochy's smack for crack –'

Sam said, 'I reckon there never was any, Vic.'

'How come?'

'Way I see it, the Yardies came down here to blow these Balkanian fuckpigs away and walk off with a load of free H.'

'What about Scrump? What was he carrying?'

'Fags and booze. Fucking boat's full of it apparently. All shrink-wrapped in plastic, straight from some warehouse or other. Scrump's French mates probably nicked it to order.'

A silence.

Vic said, 'All that for that.'

More silence.

Cromer looked back through his notes. 'What about this other RIB?'

'They'd fucked off hadn't they? Soon as they saw all the fucking fireworks they were off out of it. No lights, nothing. Unluckily for them the police boat had 'em on radar and our lads could do forty knots to their twenty –'

Vic said, 'Which direction?'

'East, back towards St Bride's and on to Portland. The lads in there –' Sam jerked his head back to the café dining room: '– had 'em in about twenty minutes. They put the searchlights on, the loudhailer – you could hear and see the whole thing from the end of the pier – our lads start to close in – bang – these Balkanian fuckpigs have only got Uzis haven't they? You can tell that fucking noise anywhere –'

'I know, we had some tonight –'

'The police boat gets riddled. You saw it – one of the flotation things shot to pieces. Our lads fire back but it's hopeless, they're sitting there half sunk, dead in the water, so the fucking Balkanians get to piss off out of it –'

'Plus the heroin?'

'If there was any, Vic. They could well have been pulling the same stunt as the fucking Yardies –'

'They wouldn't go through all that hijacking and throat-slitting for fuck-all, Sam –'

'Maybe, maybe not. They won't have got very far though – our lads say they shot the Balkanians' outboard up and it was coughing its guts out.' Sam closed his notebook. 'Anyway, that's it. Now you know as much as I do. What a fucking night –'

'Was for poor old Scrump.'

Sam shrugged. 'Wrong place, wrong time –'

Vic's mobile bipped.

The Calling Line Ident showed their home number.

Ellie's voice: 'Vic! Vic! Somebody's outside!'

Glass smashed. Ellie screamed –

36

The wall-phone crashing on kitchen tiles, then silence –

Running for the RS through the rush of panic. Sam on the café steps shouting something. Joe joining them. Cromer yelling 'It's Ellie!' at him. Everything else a blur. Sweat prickling all over. Mind blitzing with images: Ellie screaming, bleeding, falling –

Oh shit you've fucked it Hallam –

Slamming into the RS. Joe piling into the back. Cromer gunning the engine. Wheels squealing round the slipway.

Forcing his mind to slow down. 'I think they've got her, John.'

'Don't worry mate.'

Joe in the back seat. 'Anything I can do?'

'Yeah. Phone Cath.'

Fucked it, Hallam – her life, the baby, you – all for this fucking drugs crap –

Oh Christ Ellie just please don't die –

Out on to the road. A uniformed cop in a yellow traffic jacket. Stepping out into the road. Shining his torch into Cromer's eyes. Cromer wrenching the wheel. The RS thumping up the opposite kerb. 'Silly fucker.'

In Vic's wing mirror, the cop pulling his radio from his top pocket. 'You missed him John.'

Cromer grinning. 'Get him on the way back.'

Joe talking quietly to Cath on his mobile. 'When?' Listening: 'Why?'

'Slow down now. Park on the tarmac not on the gravel.'

Cromer nodded, switched off the lights, coasted up to the blank wall of the end terrace house.

Joe pocketed his mobile. 'Cath says they saw you coming back in the car. Ellie thought it was all over.'

'Fuck.'

'Said she couldn't sleep, so she went home to do some ironing and get your breakfast.'

'Right.'

Now that he could see the house, the rush of panic left him. Vic left the passenger door open and moved to the back of the terrace.

Four doors up along the narrow alley between the houses and the ragged slope of the hill against the sky, the intruder lights were on.

Oh Jesus –

The black wave engulfing him, burying him – he was going under, sinking, unable to breathe, move, see, swallow –

A long moment, leaning against the damp white-washed wall –

Coming out of it, back into the cool night air, the onshore breeze – breathing hard with relief –

Moving back to the RS, he still felt taut, keyed up – nerves like fucking piano wires for Christ sake – but now he was ice-cold, impersonal – less a man than a lump of force –

To Cromer: 'You hear what Sam was shouting?'

'Yeah. "Where's the fucking house?"'

'Joe, you take the car, tell Sam we got a hostage situation. You know the layout. Tell him we need those guys in the caff on front containment.'

'Right.'

'John, we're going in the back.'

'Right.'

'Ellie said she was going to do some ironing. The ironing board's in the kitchen, the phone's in the kitchen – I reckon that's where they've got her –'

An image of a lune at Ellie's bare neck –

As Joe climbed into the driver's seat Vic said, 'Tell Sam I reckon it's got to be the same lot shot up the police RIB – the Albanians from the hijack, maybe one or two more –'

Cromer said, 'The ones looking for you at the hospital?'

I SHALL RITERN –

'Yeah. Way I see it they've had to dump their RIB. Either at sea or on the beach –'

Cromer said, 'They wouldn't dump the heroin –'

'Fuck the heroin, John – they've got no fucking transport and every fucker's looking for 'em. They need a motor – they know Ellie's car because they followed it – they see it outside the house –'

'They're after the keys?'

'Yeah.'

Let's hope that's all they're fucking after –

He saw Cromer looking at him thinking the same –

Cromer said, 'We going in?'

'Not if we can tag 'em from outside.'

'And if we can't?'

'I go, you cover.'

'What?'

'I go, you cover. I shall need your Kevlar –'

'Fuck you talking about?'

'Don't fucking argue – I want your fucking Kevlar –'

'Why –?'

'Ellie's my wife, John.'

A silence. Staring at each other.

Cromer shrugged. 'Fair enough.' He handed the key-fob to Joe. 'Don't gun it. It's fucking noisy.'

'So I noticed.'

They watched Joe creep the RS back and roll off, no lights.

Vic said, 'We go up the hill, come down past the house, behind the lean-to. There's about a foot gap between the lean-to and the wall so we wriggle down into that, use the lean-to as cover. From there – one step to the door, two to the window.'

'Got it.'

'Watch it, it's fucking boggy behind the wall – water comes down off the hill into sedge, nettles, all kinds of shit, so don't get your fucking boots stuck. And stay right behind me, step for fucking step.'

'Yes boss.'

'Cunt.'

Cromer grinned, wrestled the Kevlar protector out of his coveralls, handed it to Vic.

'You magged up?'

'Yeah.'

'Seated?'

Cromer tapped the butt of his Glock. 'Yeah. You?'

'Yeah. Let's go.'

They had Ellie lashed to a bentwood kitchen chair with a three-metre white extension lead. Her ankles were tied to the chair's front legs, her hands behind its back.

Two dark guys in leather jackets and jeans were standing behind her. Both had Uzi submachine guns, one with a lune dangling from a strap on his wrist. A third guy, skinny, in his twenties, stood in front of Ellie, yelling at her. Spittle flew from his mouth. He had a Mazarov automatic stuck in his belt and held Ellie's steam-iron in his hand. The light in the iron's handle glowed red. The guy with the lune, burly, about forty with greying black hair, was resting the muzzle of his Uzi against the back of Ellie's neck. He was grinning and nodding at the younger guy, encouraging him. The other guy, hard-faced with pitted skin, had his Uzi trained on the door to the staircase, head cocked and listening. Vic leaned back from the broken glass panes of the door, glanced at Cromer crouching under the window. He had his Glock in his hand, barrel up, ready to go. Vic shook his head, gestured him to keep low. Cromer hunched closer under the sill.

A thudding noise: two more men, both young, came clumping down the stairs into the kitchen. Both had Uzis slung over their shoulders. They were grinning, one held his hand up, jingling Ellie's car keys. These two had jeans wet from the waist down and their muddy trainers squelched on the kitchen tiles. They must have pushed their inflatable ashore. The skinny guy standing over Ellie glanced at his watch and waved the steam-iron at the cupboard to Vic's left. A dozen cube-shaped bales were stacked against it. Each bale was about a foot across, wrapped in white polythene and bound with brown parcel tape.

If it was heroin it was worth five million quid.

The men picked up two bales each and squelched out.

Vic heard the front door open and close.

The guy with the steam-iron glanced at his watch again, and nodded. The burly guy took hold of a fistful of Ellie's curly hair and pulled her head back. The lune on his wrist hung against her cheek. Vic saw there was a red shield mark on the side of her neck where the point of the steam-iron had been touched against it. The young guy swore at her and spat in her face. Ellie glared back at him. The burly guy kept the muzzle of the Uzi at the back of her neck and leaned forward, smiling.

'He say you fuckin' English cow. He say you man kill his brother. He say now he kill you.' He grinned up at the guy with the steam-iron. 'But first he say he want fun.'

The guy held the iron close to Ellie's face. She pulled back from the heat. He muttered something to the burly guy, unzipped the fly of his jeans, pulled his prick out and began rubbing it.

'He say now you suck cock.'

'Tell him I'll bite the bugger off –'

The burly guy forced the gun muzzle into her neck, and brushed the lune against her skin, 'You do, I cut you throat, shoot you head.'

The two men with Uzis came back in, glanced at the guy rubbing his prick, grinned at each other, picked up four more bales and left. The front door opened and closed.

Vic glanced at Cromer and held up three fingers.

The burly guy pulled Ellie's head further back.

The skinny guy put the iron down upright on the table.

Vic, watching through the broken glass, held up two fingers.

The guy slapped his circumcised prick across Ellie's face.

Ellie tried to put her head down.

The burly guy pulled it back up.

Vic held up one finger.

The skinny guy's prick was now hard. He took hold of Ellie's jaw and squeezed her mouth open. All three grinning, concentrating –

Now –

'Go go go!' Vic kicked the door in.

The burly guy swung round, Uzi pointed at Vic's midriff –

The skinny guy was trying to zip himself up and pull the Mazarov at the same time –

Cromer vaulted through the kitchen window and hit the hard-faced guy in the back, sprawling him face-down on the kitchen table. A scream as his face slid into the iron –

The Uzi flared. Vic felt punches kick through the Kevlar –

Knocked backwards, he fired on automatic, watched dark wet patches travel up the burly guy's chest and then turn his face to wet red pulp –

Cromer hauled the hard-faced guy up by the hair and used the flat of his left hand to hit him hard under the nose. The taekwondo chop broke his septum and drove the bridge of his nose up into his skull. He fell to the floor, mouth open, eyes staring. His Uzi skittered across the tiles –

Vic put his boot into the skinny kid's gut. The kid pitched forward, still firing the Mazarov –

Vic watched the skinny guy squirming round on his belly, gun in hand, trying to sight on him – Vic fired the Glock –

Click–

Oh fuck – the fucking mag was empty –

He dived on to the skinny guy. Felt the breath grunt out of him. Grabbed the hand with the gun. Snapped the wrist back. The skinny guy screamed. His face twisted with rage. He spat blood in Vic's face –

A moment's disgust, then a surge of exaltation –

Got you, you fucker –

He was still smashing his fist into the guy's face when Cromer pulled him off.

'Vic – for Christ sake –'

'What –?'

'He's dead mate –'

Vic looked at the glaring wide-open eyes. 'Is he fuck –'

He tried to hit the guy again. Cromer held his arm back. 'You've gone, Vic.'

'– Talking about?' Looking at the lengths of cut extension lead hanging off the chair. 'Where's Ellie?'

'Upstairs with the medic –'

'What?' Vic tried to get to his feet. Cromer held him down.

'She's all right, Vic –'

'Let me fucking go will you –'

Cromer held on to his shoulders and shook him till his head spun. 'You went, mate. You lost it.'

'What –?'

'You went apeshit.'

'What about the other two?'

'They ran out with the stuff. Joe was waiting for 'em –'

'*Joe?*'

'Yeah. He led the police van over here –'

'Fucking hell – all I told him to do was tell Sam –'

'Told me he was so pissed off about Scrump, the boat, you, Ellie, every fucking thing – he said he just got fired up –'

'Oh shit –'

'Anyway, he gets here first, jumps out the RS, sees the two guys loading up Ellie's car, watches 'em come back in here and hides behind the car. The two guys pick up the second load – they're carrying two bales each, no hands free, guns on their backs . . . Joe's hiding behind the car – they start loading up and Joe slams the boot down on 'em, grabs 'em by the scruff and wallop, bangs their heads together – end of story. One of 'em's still out cold. Then – guess what –'

'What?'

'Joe throws up. He's out there now, sitting on the front steps, weak as a kitten.' Cromer shook his head. 'He actually wept, Vic. Big bloke like that and he was sobbing his fucking heart out. He says that's the effect it has on him –'

'Yeah. Always has done, since he was a kid . . . Sooner take it out on a lump of metal –'

'Maybe that's the best way to be –'

'Yeah, maybe –'

'Least you don't get all that fucking counselling.'

Cromer grinned. 'Because that's what you've got to look forward to –'

Vic realised Cromer was trying to take his mind off it, talk him down, get him to move forward. It wasn't what he wanted: there was something else he needed to know: 'John – did you enjoy it?'

'What?'

'When you offed those blokes in Palmer Street.'

Cromer took his time, gazing round the blood-spattered floor and walls: '. . . I don't know about enjoying it, Vic. I thought they had it coming.' A shrug and a crooked grin. 'I thought I was doing the right thing. Committing justice.'

Vic said, 'I didn't. I fucking enjoyed it . . . After watching what the cunt was trying to do to Ellie, I couldn't wait to fucking hammer him.'

'Fuck sake don't tell your counsellors that.'

'It was a release, John. After being pissed about all night – that fucking lorry, those kids in the container, here, seeing Ellie – that guy was a big fucking prize, a gift. "You, I thought, you're mine. Thank you –"'

'Yeah but that's only how you feel at the time –'

'Too fucking dangerous, mate – it's insane –'

'Yeah.' Cromer felt the edge of his left hand. 'Some fucker's trying to kill you, what can you do?'

They looked at each other. Vic said, 'Can you get my fags out? My hands are too fucking swollen.'

'Yeah, where?'

'Top left-hand pocket.'

'Right –'

'Thanks.' Vic lit up. 'Was it heroin in the bales?'

'Yeah. Sixty kilos.'

'Sam'll be pleased.'

Cromer helped Vic lumber to his feet. His arms and legs were shaking and his whole body ached. He saw his reddened fists bore the guy's teethmarks; even his forearms were slimed with warm blood. 'How long was I at him –?'

'Not long – the Marine guys came straight in.'

'I don't remember a fucking thing.' Now he was washing his hands in the stainless-steel sink. The bowl was full of broken glass from the window. The water ran rusty-brown over the shards.

Cromer handed him a length of paper kitchen towel. 'Wipe that blood and gob off your mush.'

Vic splashed cold water over his face and hair. He blotted himself dry, looked at his hands. They were still quivering.

'I've had this, John.'

Cromer said, 'Yeah well. It takes a time.' He put his left hand under the cold tap; the red mark was already turning into a grey-blue bruise. 'I don't know how fucking long though.'

Vic went up to see Ellie. She was drowsy and said she'd been given painkillers and something for shock. Vic saw the medic had taped a square of gauze to the shield mark on her neck; she had red lines from the extension lead round her wrists and ankles. Vic straightened the duvet over her and sat holding her hand until her eyelids fluttered and closed. They had a blue-violet tint; he sat beside her, equally exhausted. Then, as he watched her, he felt love, fierce and primal, begin to pump and flood out of him, protecting her. Slowly, her mouth relaxed into its familiar sleeping smile.

Please God let them be all right.